THE HOLLOW PRESIDENT

PHILIP CAINE

THE HOLLOW PRESIDENT

First paperback edition printed 2017 in the United Kingdom

ISBN 9780993374838

Published by REDOAK
philcaine777@hotmail.com
For more copies of this book, please email the above.

Editing & Critique: Gillian Ogilvie
Technical Editor: Malcolm Caine

Cover Design: www.gonzodesign.co.uk
Main Cover Photo: www.pixaby.com

Printed in Great Britain by:
Orbital Print

http://philcaine777.wix.com/philipcaine

ABOUT THE AUTHOR

Philip has over thirty five years' experience operating projects across 3 continents, within the Oil & Gas Industry, providing support in facilitates & project management.

His career began in hotel management and then transitioned to offshore North Sea, where he worked the boom years on Oil Rigs, Barges & Platforms. Seventeen years passed and Philip returned to onshore projects taking a three year contract to manage accommodation bases in North & West Africa.

From Africa Philip moved to the 'Former Soviet Union' where he directed multiple projects in Kazakhstan & Russia, a particularly exciting seven years where dealings with the KGB were an everyday event.

The end of the Iraq War in 2003 took Philip to Baghdad where, as Operations Director, he controlled the operations & management of multiple accommodation bases for the American Military. A challenging location that required him to deliver full support for over 30,000 troops, on nine locations throughout the city. He left Baghdad in 2010.

The last three years of his career were spent running a couple of support services companies in Iraq with head offices in Dubai.

Philip semi-retired in 2014 and began writing in February 2015 after joining Ulverston Writers Group. His first novel, PICNIC IN IRAQ, is an adventure treasure hunt set in Iraq. The sequel, TO CATCH A FOX, is an exciting rescue mission set in Syria. BREAKFAST IN BEIRUT, sees the main character, Jack Castle, working for MI6 in the Middle East.

THE HOLLOW PRESIDENT is his forth novel.

Also by Philip Caine

'The Jack Castle Series'

PICNIC IN IRAQ

TO CATCH A FOX

BREAKFAST IN BEIRUT

"Power tends to corrupt, and absolute power corrupts absolutely.
Great men are almost always bad, almost always hollow."

Lord Acton, 1887 . . .

THE HOLLOW PRESIDENT

Prologue
March 2005

East of Kabul, the watery sunlight sparkled on the snow-covered peaks of the Paghman Mountains. At the controls of the C130 aircraft, Captain Mark Waterman spoke into the mic, 'Hercules-901, Bagram control, request permission to take-off.'

'Bagram control, Hercules-901, you are clear for take-off on Romeo-Two.'

'Thank you, Bagram.'

The four engines purred as the big cargo plane lumbered onto the end of the runway. Waterman pushed the throttles to maximum and felt the control column shudder as the huge turbines roared into life. As the aircraft left the tarmac, the captain pulled hard back on the controls and banked to the south in a steady climb over the mountains that surrounded the ancient city.

The small fire had kept the man's hands warm and fingers nimble. Through powerful binoculars he'd watched the plane move to the runway and climb into the clear morning sky. He'd prepared the weapon and checked it several times while waiting for the Hercules to leave the airbase. He lifted the cumbersome launcher to his shoulder and braced himself as the aircraft headed towards his position. His breath swirled around his head as he exhaled, then his finger gently squeezed the trigger.

The rocket shot skyward, the vapour trail white in its wake, screaming towards the target.

'Incoming! Incoming!' yelled Waterman.

The co-pilot fired the counter measures but it was too late. The ground-to-air missile struck between the first and second engines and the wing, loaded with fuel, added to the explosion.

The man eased the heavy launcher from his shoulder and watched as the huge fireball engulfed the doomed aircraft.

Chapter One
June 2011
'Charlie Webster'

Jack Castle drove slowly up the shrub-lined approach to his Berkshire home. He parked the sleek Jaguar next to Nicole's 4x4 and walked around to the rear of the property. The afternoon was warm and he could hear his wife and daughters giggling on the back lawn. As he turned the corner he stopped for a few seconds and watched as the three played on a big rug.

'Hello, ladies.'

The twins turned and beamed at the sound of his voice. 'Daddy's home,' said Nicole.

The two little one-year-olds trotted to meet him, delight on their faces, as his wife stood and followed them. Scooping up the girls he kissed their cheeks, 'How are my little angels?'

Nicole put her arms around her family, then leaned in to kiss her husband. Jack could smell her perfume as she pressed her lips against his.

The nanny came through the patio doors. 'Phone for you, Mr. Jack.'

He put the girls down and took the handset. 'Thanks, Svetlana. Hello?'

'Jack? This is Maggie Webster. Charlie's wife.'

'Hello, Maggie. How are you? How's Charlie? Everything okay?'

'No, Jack. Charlie's dying.'

'Oh, no. I'm so sorry.'

'He's asking to see you. He says it's very important. Can you come?'

'Yes, of course. I'm heading out to the Middle East tomorrow but I'll be back in about a week.'

'He hasn't got that long, Jack.'

'Right, yes. Okay, I'll come up today. You guys still in Cheshire?'

'Yes.'

'Okay, what's your postcode, Maggie?'

Jack took out his smart phone and tapped in the code. 'I'll leave within the hour and be there soon as I can.'

'Thank you, Jack. See you later.'

Nicole frowned. 'What is it, darling?'

'One of my old army buddies is dying.'

'Oh, I'm sorry.'

'I need to go up to Cheshire, Nikki. He wants to see me. Apparently it's important.'

'Yes, of course. You must go, Zaikin.'

'If I leave now, I can be back tonight. Sorry, babe.'

'Don't be silly. Go. And drive safely. I love you.'

'Love you too,' he bent down and kissed the twins, then went into the house.

It took a little under three hours for Jack to make the drive to Cheshire and it was almost six o'clock when he pulled into the driveway of the Tudor-style house in the elegant village of Mottram St Andrew. As he climbed out of the Jag, the front door opened and a gaunt looking Maggie came out to meet him. 'Hello, Jack. Thank you so much for coming.'

16

As they hugged Jack said, 'No problem. Where is he?'

'We moved his bed into the study, so he could see the garden. This way.'

As they entered the room Jack said, 'He's sleeping?'

At the bedside Maggie gently touched her husband's shoulder. 'Jack is here, darling.'

Charlie Webster opened his bloodshot eyes and smiled weakly at his old friend, 'Hello, Jack.'

'Maggie bent down and kissed his forehead. 'I'll leave you boys to talk. Please don't tire him. Can I get you a drink, Jack?'

Jack shook his head and she left the room. 'No point asking how you're doing, buddy.'

Charlie sucked in a deep breath. The rasping sound as it entered his lungs made Jack wince. 'Can I get you anything?'

Another gasp of breath and the dying man slowly shook his head. 'Jack, thanks for coming.'

'No problem. What can I do for you, Charlie?'

'Kabul, two thousand and three. A Hercules was shot down,' he paused, eyes closed, then coughed weakly.

Jack put his hand on his friend's chest. 'Take your time, mate.'

The bloodshot eyes slowly opened. 'You know the one I'm talking about? It was supposed to be loaded with captured opium?'

'Yeah, I remember. Something like sixty or seventy tons of raw opium had been taken from the Taliban. The Americans were gonna ship it to Bahrain, or somewhere?'

17

'That's right. Thing is, the plane they shot down, didn't have any opium on-board.'

Jack stood up and took a bottle of mineral water from the side table. 'Do you mind?'

'Charlie nodded slightly.'

'So what happened to the opium?'

Another rasping breath was followed by a weak cough. 'It was switched, Jack. They switched the opium to another flight. They shot that plane down themselves, to cover the theft of seventy tons of raw opium.'

'Who did, Charlie? Who took the cargo?'

'A lot of senior men were involved. But the man in charge was General Alexander Stonewall Mason.'

Jack's mouth opened slightly and Charlie saw the surprise on his old friend's face. 'That's right Jack, the general that was, and is now, President Elect, Alex Mason.'

'Charlie, are you sure? You're saying the guy who is gonna be the next president of the United States masterminded a billion dollar opium heist?'

'That's right, Jack.'

Chapter Two
'Phone Calls'

For over two hours Jack listened to Charlie talking on and off, as his friend slipped in and out of a medicated sleep. Maggie had insisted he was left to rest but each time he woke he was adamant his friend needed to know more of the story. It was after eight-thirty when Jack left Mottram St Andrew.

His thoughts on the drive back to Berkshire were filled with the amazing tale he'd been told. The dossier Charlie had kept was filled with names, dates, photocopies of orders and several newspaper cuttings and although Jack had only flipped through the contents, it certainly looked like the information therein corroborated the dying man's story. As he drove south down the busy M6 motorway he glanced at the leather document case on the seat beside him, his thoughts racing, *I need to get this to Mathew. This is dynamite.*

Mathew Sterling was Jack's younger brother. They'd grown up in the north of England, in a beautiful home on the edge of Lake Windermere. In his mid-fifties, Jack Castle was tall, reasonably fit and healthy. Greying hair complemented sparkling brown eyes that gave a light to his tanned face. He had a good sense of humour and an infectious personality which appealed to most people. His parents had tragically died in a car accident on his twentieth birthday and it was this which caused Jack to

19

abandon the idea of following in his father's footsteps and becoming a doctor, electing instead to join the British Army. He'd spent fifteen years in the military trying to overcome the guilt and anger he harboured following the death of his parents. He'd worked hard and rose to the rank of captain in the Special Air Service, after which he'd moved into the world of private security. The company he'd joined back then now belonged to him and with the help of his partner and friend, Tom Hillman, they had grown the business into a respected international entity.

His brother Mathew also entered the military but had taken a different path. He'd initially worked in Military Intelligence and spent many years as a field operative for MI6. He rose quickly through the security service and now, based in London's Vauxhall Cross building, he was section chief of the Middle East desk. For security reasons he had chosen to use his mother's maiden name and for the last twenty years had been known as Mr. Mathew Sterling.

Jack tapped the small screen in the centre of the dash board. When the display read TELEPHONE, Jack cleared his throat and said clearly, 'Call Mathew.'

'Hello, Jack. How're you doing?'

'Mathew, hi there. I've just been up to Cheshire to see an old buddy of mine. I'm on my way home now but I could do with talking to you, bro?'

'Sure. Tomorrow morning okay, or does it have to be this evening?'

'I'm still on the M6, so tomorrow is fine, Matt.'

'Okay, see you about eleven-ish?'

'Yeah, see you then.'

Jack tapped the display to end the call and noticed the time. *One o'clock in the morning in Dubai.* In a clear voice he said, 'Call Tom.'

Tom Hillman was not only Jack's business partner, he was his closest friend. They had served in the army together and been friends for over twenty years. He was a few years younger than Jack, slightly shorter and slimmer, with close cropped fair hair, tanned face and blue eyes. Originally born and raised in the UK, he spent most of his younger life in Leeds but his home now was Dubai, where he lived with his wife, Helen. The latter years of Tom's military career had been spent in Military Intelligence and the skills learned during that time had proved to be invaluable on more than one occasion.

Several seconds and as many beeps later, Tom Hillman's sleepy voice came over the speaker. 'Jack, what's up, mate?'

'Tom. Sorry to wake you, buddy.'

'It's okay. What's up?'

'Something's come up. I'm not gonna get down to Dubai tomorrow. Do you mind handling the meetings yourself?'

'Yeah, sure. The meetings are no problem. What's happened? Can I help?'

'I'm meeting Mathew in the morning. I'll talk to you later in the day.'

'Okay, mate. Anything else?'

'No, that's it. Go back to sleep.'

'Yeah, cheers. Take care buddy.'

Jack tapped the screen to end the call, waited a few seconds and said, 'Call Nicole.'

'Zaikin, everything okay?'

'Hi, darling, yeah I'm fine. Be home in a couple hours. You don't need to wait up.'

'You're leaving for Dubai tomorrow. I'll wait.'

'Change of plan, Nikki, I'm not going tomorrow.'

'Oh, good, but I'll still wait up. Drive carefully.'

'Okay, see you soon. Love you.'

Chapter Three
'The Story'

It was a few minutes before eleven when Jack entered Vauxhall Cross, the home of the British Secret Service. Although Jack continued to operate his own company, he'd been seconded a year ago to undertake ad-hoc missions for MI6, especially in the Middle East. He flashed his ID to the burly officer at the door and then laid the leather folder and the contents of his pockets on the x-ray machine conveyor belt, collecting them a few seconds later on the other side of the security scanner. The short ride in the lift had him at the door of his brother's office as Big Ben struck eleven o'clock.

Mathew's secretary stood as Jack entered the outer office. 'Good morning, Mr. Castle.'

Jack smiled. 'Morning, Victoria. How's the motorbike? You still speeding through the streets of London?'

The girl blushed slightly. 'Always, sir. You can go straight in. Can I get you a drink?'

'Nothing for me, thank you.'

Jack knocked on the door and walked in without waiting to be called. Mathew Sterling was at the window looking out over the River Thames, his smartphone to his ear. He waved to Jack to take a seat. A few minutes later Sterling finished the call and turned to his brother. 'Sorry about that,' he said smiling. 'How you doing, Jack? How are Nicole and my beautiful nieces?'

Jack returned the smile. 'All good. A hand-full, but all good.'

'Do you want something to drink?'

'No, I just had some, thanks.'

Mathew pressed the intercom. 'Victoria?'

'Sir?'

'Tea for one please. And, unless it's the Director General please hold my calls.

'Yes, sir.'

'Right, Jack. I'm all ears.'

Over an hour later, Mathew stood up and returned to the window. 'My God. This is incredible.'

They had gone through the contents of Charlie Webster's folder and both agreed the story the dying man had given Jack was totally corroborated in the file's contents.

Mathew turned from the window. 'So General Mason and his chums stole a billion and a half dollars-worth of raw opium and sold it to the Russian Mafia.'

'Looks like it, Matt. The plane was supposed to fly the cargo to Bahrain and from there, ship it to a legitimate pharmaceuticals company in Hong Kong.'

Mathew pressed the intercom.

'Sir?'

'Victoria, bring in some more tea please. And an extra cup.'

'Yes, sir'

He looked at his brother. 'The thing I don't understand, Jack, is why Webster didn't come forward before now?'

'He was paid a quarter of a million to fly the opium to Russia. And now people are being murdered, so I guess he thought he'd make amends before he died?'

A knock on the door stopped the conversation.'

'Come.'

'Tea, sir.'

'Thank you, Victoria.'

Mathew poured two cups and Jack joined him at the table. 'Charlie took the money, but didn't know they planned to blow up the cargo plane. Or indeed murder anyone.'

The MI6 chief frowned. 'Bit naive isn't it? What did he think was going to happen?'

Jack picked up his cup. 'Yes, in retrospect it was. But now, since the general is going to be the next president, it certainly looks like someone is killing off anyone who was involved.'

Mathew took a sheet of paper from Webster's folder and quickly read down the list of conspirators again . . .

Charles Anthony Webster; British Security Consultant
General Alexander Stonewall Mason; US Army; Retired
Colonel James Stubbs; US Army; <u>Killed in car accident</u>
Colonel David Hendricks; US Army; Retired
Colonel Jasper Mickelson; US Logistics Corp; Retired
Colonel Marcus Nelson; US Military Intelligence
Major Thomas O'Malley; <u>Killed in skiing accident</u>
Major Gregory Schaffer; <u>Died in drowning accident</u>
Captain Anders Bergen; Serving, Andrews Air Base

He looked up from the document and said, 'There are nine names on this list, including the general and your pal Charlie. It says here, three are already dead.'

Jack took the list. 'Let's assume the general, sorry, President Elect Mason and his cronies, knew Charlie was dying, that leaves four more people to bump off.'

Mathew took a sip of tea. 'Yes, and our next question is, what do we do about this?'

'We go after this guy. That's what we do?'

Mathew smiled. 'This, guy, as you call him, is going to be the next President of the United States of America.'

'He's a murderer and a thief, Matt. Maybe not by his own hand but he masterminded the Bagram switch and is now killing off anyone who was involved. Not to mention the four aircrew that died.'

'Yes, Jack, I do understand all that but we must proceed very carefully.' Sterling looked out the window again. 'I want to talk to Charlie Webster myself. Then I'll speak with the Director General, who will most certainly want to talk to the Foreign Secretary, if not the PM.'

Jack nodded. 'Okay, let's get up to Cheshire. I'm calling Charlie's wife now.'

Mathew pressed the intercom.

'Sir?'

'Come in please, Victoria.'

A few seconds later the secretary entered. 'Sir?'

'I need a car and out-rider immediately. Destination is Cheshire. Mottram St Andrew.'

'Very good, sir.'

Jack ended the call and turned to the girl. 'That won't be necessary, Victoria.'

'Sorry, sir?'

Jack looked at his brother. 'Charlie Webster died last night.'

Chapter Four
'The DG Meeting'

They'd been waiting for over twenty minutes when the intercom beeped. Gareth, the Director General's secretary, said, 'She's ready for you now, gentlemen.'

They stood as the young man knocked and opened the door. 'Mr Sterling and Mr Castle, ma'am.'

'Thank you, Gareth. Come in, gentlemen.'

As the brothers entered, the elegant woman behind the desk stood and walked towards them. Offering her hand she said, 'Good to see you again, Jack. How is your lovely family?'

'Nice to see you too, ma'am. And yes, they're all well.'

No handshake was given to Sterling, instead she touched him lightly on the shoulder. 'Let's have a seat, Mathew.'

'Thank you, ma'am.'

Jack placed Charlie's folder on the table between them. 'Thank you for seeing me at such short notice, ma'am.'

'Not at all. Mathew tells me you have something important.' She leaned forward and tapped the leather folder. 'It's all in here I take it?'

'That's correct. You need to go through this urgently, ma'am.'

The woman smiled. 'Why not give me a brief overview first, Jack?'

Thirty minutes later the DG stood and went to her desk and clicked the intercom. 'Gareth?'

The metallic voice came back. 'Yes, ma'am?'

'Tea for three please,' she turned from the desk and looked out the window. 'This is extremely sensitive. And to be honest, somewhat circumstantial.'

Jack stood. 'With respect, ma'am, it's all here in the folder. Names, dates, the deaths, the reports.'

The DG raised her hand. 'Sit down please, Jack, and listen for a second.'

Mathew looked at his brother and nodded to the couch.

The knock on the door eased the slight tension in the room. 'Come,'

After the secretary left the room Mathew reached for the tea tray. 'I'll be mother.'

The Director took her seat in the big leather chair. 'What we have here, gentlemen, is a bundle of documents that do no more than report on an incident in Afghanistan; and a series of murders. Yes, it does implicate President Elect Mason but it is indeed all circumstantial. We do not have any real proof.'

'Charlie Webster was there ma'am. He knew what happened.'

The woman put down her teacup, a slightly exasperated look on her face. 'I'm sure he did, Jack. But unfortunately Mr Webster is no longer with us.'

'So we're going to do nothing?'

'I never said that. We have a couple of options. One, we hand this over to our cousins in the American Embassy and let them pass it onto the FBI. Two, we go directly to the FBI. Three, we do nothing, as it is an

American issue and nothing to do with the British security services.'

Jack stood again, clearly annoyed at the way the conversation was going. 'I'm afraid, and again with respect, I can't sit back and do nothing, ma'am.'

The woman smiled. 'I wouldn't expect you to, Jack.'

'Ma'am?'

'A man like you would want to go and get the proof. And prove that all this really is the work of Alexander Mason. Wouldn't he?'

'Yes, I would.'

'Of course you would. It's just a pity I can't order you to get involved on behalf of the British Government.'

Jack smiled at the Director, his eyes narrowed. 'But there is nothing to stop me investigating this myself?'

'Oh, I couldn't possibly comment on that. Jack. But I'm sure you'll make the right decision on what to do with this dossier and where to go to find some solid evidence.' The DG stood up. 'Now if you'll excuse me, gentlemen, I have to be in Downing Street in an hour.'

Jack smiled and offered his hand. 'Thank you, ma'am.'

'Not at all, Jack. Mathew, everything else under control?'

'Yes, ma'am. All under control.'

'Well done. Good afternoon, gentlemen.'

As they were leaving the room the woman said, 'Good luck with your endeavours, Mr. Castle. And be careful.'

It was late afternoon when Jack left Vauxhall Cross. The meeting with the Director General had not gone as Jack hoped but it did give him the leeway to undertake 'enquiries' himself. He and Mathew had discussed a broad plan, which would allow Jack to operate under his own volition. Mathew would provide support and assistance when required, albeit covertly. It was understood, in the event of anything compromising Jack's mission, the British Government would deny all knowledge of his actions. The security of Charlie Webster's dossier was a concern, so all the documents had been scanned and saved digitally onto Jack's smartphone. The original folder was now safely locked away in Mathew's office safe.

The train journey from Central London to Berkshire took just over fifty minutes and gave Jack the opportunity to go over the plan again. By the time he arrived at East Monkton station, he was confident he could discover the truth about the Bagram heist and the general's involvement. He left the train and nodded to the platform attendant as he passed through the gate and out to the small car park. The Jaguar lights blinked as he unlocked the car. Inside he sat for several seconds thinking about the conversation with Charlie. *What was it he said about the flight that went to Russia?*

Jack pressed the start button and the powerful engine gurgled into life, ten minutes later he pulled up in front of his house. After parking the car he stood for several seconds and looked up at the beautiful house and the home he and Nicole had made for themselves. *Was he willing to risk it all for something that really did not concern him? Of course he was.*

Chapter Five
'One More Fish'

Eighty miles west of Washington DC, close to the small town of Brandley, is a secluded but extremely beautiful stretch of water known to the locals as Summerlake.

The bright red canoe reflected in the mirror-like water as David Hendricks watched his twelve year old grandson expertly attach the bait to the hook. 'It'll be dark in an hour, so this'll be our last fish,' said the old man.

The boy flipped the weighted line several yards from the canoe, turned and smiled. 'Okay, gran'pa, just one more fish.'

The sun had set behind the tree-covered mountains in West Virginia and the warmth of the day had slipped away by the time they paddled the canoe up to the small jetty. Hendricks pulled in the holding net and let the water drain away to reveal five wriggling fish. The boy jumped onto the jetty and secured the canoe, then took the net from his grandfather. After collecting the equipment they walked up the short banking to the log cabin. 'Fish for supper, Bobby.'

'Again!' replied the boy.

They both laughed.

It was dark when they finished supper. The boy went to bed early, tired after the busy morning in the woods and the afternoon on the lake. Hendricks smiled contentedly to himself as he sat on the veranda, the crescent moon illuminating the beautiful lake. He smoked a fat Monte Cristo and relished the taste and aroma from the expensive cigar. An occasional fish disturbed the stillness, as it nipped a firefly from the surface of the flat water.

He finished his cigar and stubbed out the butt in an overflowing ashtray, then walked to the steps. He strained his ears but heard nothing from the surrounding woods. *Very strange, no sound at all,* he thought, then turned and went into the cabin.

A few days later the front page of the Virginia Tribune read, *RETIRED COLONEL DIES.* The by-line gave a short career history of the retired soldier, followed by a brief report on the tragic death of the man and his twelve year old grandson. The pair were believed to have succumbed to a gas leak while sleeping. The provisional coroner's report indicated a faulty valve on the stove's butane cylinder, resulting in the accidental death of the victims.

* * *

In Washington, President Elect Alex Mason was chairing an oversight committee on security budgeting, when his smartphone vibrated in his pocket. Discreetly he slipped the phone from his Jacket and swiped the screen. He scrolled through the Tribune's report on the death of his old comrade until he found the coroner's verdict. As he placed the phone on the desk, his aid was curious as to why the senator was smiling in such a serious meeting.

Chapter Six
'Donny'

On the sun-bathed patio, Jack had the cup to his mouth. The twins giggled at the funny noises he made as he slurped the tea, much to the displeasure of Nicole, 'Don't laugh at daddy girls. He's very naughty making that noise.'

Jack's cross-eyed look turned the giggles to laughter.

'Zaikin, behave.'

More funny faces from Jack brought more delighted laughter from his daughters. He stood and went round the table, kissed each of the girls and then Nicole. 'Sorry, mummy. Daddy is very naughty,' which only resulted in even more laughter from the beautiful twins.

The nanny came out. 'Mr Jack. Your car is here now.'

'Thanks, Svetlana. Tell him I'll just be a few minutes, please.'

'Call me before you take off, Zaikin, and when you get to Kabul.'

Jack smiled. 'Don't I always?' he put his arms around her and pulled her close, 'I love you.'

She turned her face up to his, and kissed him gently. 'Be careful. I love you.'

The kissing brought on yet another fit of giggles from the girls.

The chauffer car took almost an hour to get to Heathrow, which gave Jack the opportunity to think about the next few days. He had no doubt what he was doing was right, but was it wise? *Take on the next president of the United States . . . Yeah, fuck it.*

He picked up his wheelie and thanked the driver; entered the Business Class Departures and went straight to security. Jack flashed his smartphone to the big man at the desk, who took it and scanned the online boarding pass. Following a speedy screening, he was in the business lounge in less than ten minutes after arriving. He helped himself to a couple of Danish pastries and a mug of tea and found a seat by the big windows overlooking the tarmac. As he sat down a smart businesswoman looked up from her laptop and smiled.

He returned the smile and said, 'Good morning,' then tucked into his Danish.

The lounge was as busy as usual, but there appeared to be no delays and, according to the Departures Board, all flights were on-time. He took out his phone, checked messages and emails, then made several calls; the last one to his old friend in Afghanistan, Donny Murray.

The flight to Kabul was tedious and the ninety minute wait in Istanbul did nothing to improve Jack's mood. The good thing was he would get to meet up with his friend Donny. Although they had stayed in touch, they'd not seen each other for over fifteen years.

The turbulence as the big Turkish Airways plane descended over the mountains was unpleasant to say the least, with many of the local passengers uttering prayers to whichever God they worshipped. As the aircraft levelled out at one thousand feet, the turbulence subsided. Smiles returned to the faces of the more fearful passengers, as the pilot eased the plane gently onto the tarmac.

The grandly named, Kabul International Airport, belies the true condition of this ageing, antiquated facility. Built in the 60's by Russian engineers and then bombed by the coalition in 2002 the airport is a testament to the unstable nature of this ravaged country. The main terminal has been rebuilt and although functional, still remains unwelcoming.

After a laborious Passport Control and an equally unnecessary search at Customs, Jack exited the building and boarded a crowded and smelly courtesy bus to the outer security checkpoint. A final procedure to check entry documents was undertaken again and, almost an hour after landing, Jack walked out of the airport's main exit.

The melee of people waiting outside was a mixture of family and friends collecting loved ones, taxi drivers touting for business, street vendors offering cheap souvenirs, and children begging. He stood on the top step and scanned the throng until he saw Donny, both arms in the air and standing well back from the crowd. Jack descended the unsafe, broken steps and pushed past the taxi drivers, each pulling at his bag, hoping for his business. Moving to the side he escaped the thick of it, but was quickly pursued by the urchin beggars. Donny came to his rescue scattering a handful of coins into the road; the delighted children scrambled for the money like a swarm of flies on a discarded cheeseburger.

They quickly shook hands and after a swift embrace, moved away from the madness and out to the car park.

'Good to see you again, Jack. You're looking well mate.'

'You too, buddy. It's been a while.'

'Yeah, where do all the years go?'

The hazard lights blinked on a Russian-made Volga, as Donny unlocked the vehicle.

'Great car, mate,' said Jack, 'I love these.'

'Yeah, there are a lot of them in Kabul, so it's a bit safer and far less conspicuous than driving around in an armoured 4x4.'

Donny opened the boot and took out a set of body-armour. Jack placed his bag in the boot, took off his Jacket and slipped the protection over his head, fastening it securely around his torso. After putting his Jacket back on, he climbed into the passenger seat. As Donny started the engine Jack looked through the dusty window. 'Back in the bad-lands.'

His old friend turned and grinned. 'Aint that the truth!'

Chapter Seven
'Bagram'

The roads of the old city were busy as ever and progress through the streets was slow.

'Bad time of the day,' said Donny, 'Friday prayers over and the mosques are emptying.'

'I don't know how you've done it for so many years, mate. I've been in some shit places but driving round Kabul must be the most dangerous. At least in Baghdad we had decent roads we could rock-n-roll on.'

They were travelling no more than fifteen miles an hour when the explosion shocked them into silence. Donny instinctively hit the brakes as the huge crimson fireball filled the street a hundred yards in front.

'Oh fuck,' said Jack.

'Jesus,' said Donny as he slipped the gears into reverse. 'Hold on, mate.'

Backing up onto the pavement, he reversed the big car along the busy sidewalk as shocked locals cursed and jumped out of the way. The evening wind blew the acrid black smoke along the crowded street, choking and blinding the panicked locals. Donny had the car moving quickly backwards now; the side street only ten yards away.

'We'll be outta here in a . . .'

A second, larger explosion cut short his words as the vehicle bumped off the kerb and back onto the road. He spun the wheel and reversed down the narrow side street, startling an old donkey that broke free from its tether and bolted into an open shop doorway. A few seconds later they were at the next corner of the block. Donny spun the car in a one-eighty, put the car into drive and accelerated away from the danger zone.

'A warm welcome, eh?' said Jack.

Donny grinned. 'Not exactly what I'd planned.'

They looked at each other and laughed.

Jack had met Donny Murray almost thirty years ago when they were recruits at the army training camp in Catterick, Northern England. There was a pub where military and civilians used to go to knock lumps out of each other, and it was here Donny had saved Jack from a good kicking, when three of the locals had decided to use a drunken Jack Castle as a punch-bag. The two men had been friends ever since. Born in Manchester, Donny was now in his early fifties, as tall as Jack, but slimmer and certainly fitter. He worked as Country Manager for an American company that provided security on the huge fuel depot at Bagram Air Base, a position he had taken as a twelve month contract, but had lasted for over ten years.

The drive from Kabul airport to the Bagram base had taken longer than expected thanks to the explosions in the city, and the emergency checkpoints on all roads out of town. It was almost sunset when the Volga pulled up to the outer security gate at Bagram. Donny flashed his ID and Jack handed over his passport and American Department of Defence badge. The guard checked the documents, while a second man walked round the car with a sniffer-dog. A third guard, with the aid of a large mirror on wheels, looked under the vehicle. Inspection over, their documents were passed back and the Volga was waved forward to the main gate into the air base. The big steel portal slid back and the vehicle slowly moved forward and up to the internal security check. ID's were scrutinised once more and the vehicle was allowed to proceed.

Donny turned to Jack. 'Welcome to Bagram, mate.'

They drove at five miles an hour and, a few minutes after entering the base, pulled up in the parking area of Donny's accommodation building. 'This block houses all our company staff. I've got you a room on the second floor with the management team.'

'Sounds good to me,' said Jack, as he collected his bag.

They entered the reception area and were greeted by a young man seated behind a small desk.

'Evening, Mike,' said Donny, 'this is Mr Castle. He'll be with us a day or two. He'll be in 201.'

'Okay, boss.' The man stood and prepared an electronic key-card. Handing it to Jack he said, 'This will get you into the building, and your room. You can also use it in the canteen to purchase your meals. Security procedures are in your room and there is, as I'm sure you have noticed, an emergency bunker at each end of the building. '

Jack smiled and took the card, 'Thanks, Mike.'

Donny slapped Jack on the back, 'Okay, get settled in and I'll meet you back here in an hour.'

The two friends had dined together in the service company canteen and it was dark as they walked back to the accommodation block. Donny sat in the chair next to his desk, drinking from a can of beer. Jack, on the couch, sipped from a large mug of steaming tea.

Donny leaned back in the chair and put his feet up on the desk. 'Okay, me old mate, what's this all about?'

Chapter Eight
'Kamenka'

The two old friends had talked into the early hours of the morning, first about the issue at hand and what they would do to gather more information; then reminiscences from years gone by. Donny Murray had been in Afghanistan for over ten years and had an excellent contact base throughout the region. His company not only provided security for fuel coming into the country, but actually provided all the fuel used by the coalition. Any aircraft leaving a coalition airbase in the last ten years would have been fuelled by Donny's company, which meant he had access to the records of all flights. They were now on their way to the military side of Kabul Airport, to see one of Murray's managers.

The ride from Bagram to Kabul had thankfully been uneventful and it was mid-morning by the time they entered the coalition base. After passing through the stringent security area, they were met by Mike Sanderson, Donny's manager. Sanderson and Donny had worked together in Mogadishu and when Murray had been head-hunted for the Country Manager's position in Afghanistan, Sanderson had come with him.

'Morning Mike,' said Donny, 'this is a good friend of mine, Jack Castle.'

Offering his hand, Jack said, 'Good to meet you, Mike.'

As they shook hands the manager smiled. 'Pleasure to meet you too, Jack. Not often one gets to meet a legend.'

Jack grinned, 'Err . . . I don't know about legend.'

'Donny's spoken about you on several occasions.'

Jack looked at his old friend. 'All exaggerated I'm sure.'

'Okay, gentlemen, what can I do for you?'

Donny put his arm around Mike's shoulder. 'First a cuppa coffee. Then we need to take a look at your records, mate.'

The staff had gone to lunch and Jack, Donny and Mike were in the operations office checking the data base on the day the cargo plane, allegedly carrying the opium, had been shot down. Mike expertly scrolled through numerous fuel consumption logs, aircraft identity info and basic cargo. There had been over seventy flights on the day the C130 was destroyed, but it only took Mike fifteen minutes to identify a flight that appeared to look out of the ordinary.

Mike pointed to the screen. 'Take a look at this.'

Donny leaned in and said, 'Civilian charter?'

Mike highlighted the information on the screen and hit the print button. He collected the printout from the machine and checked it was what he wanted, returned to the computer, closed down the programme and deleted the access history. Waving the document he said, 'Let's go to my office before the guys get back from lunch.'

As they entered Mike's office, he turned to his secretary, 'I'll be in a meeting for the next hour, Stacy.'

'Okay, Mike.'

'Have a seat, guys. Anything to drink?'

'Just water please,' said Jack.

'Same for me please,' said Donny, 'So what about this civilian charter?'

Mike took the drinks from a small fridge, passed them out, and then sat down at his desk. 'Hold on, let me look at this.' A few minutes later he raised his head. 'Looks like it's been a civilian charter requested by the military to move medical supplies.'

Jack finished his water. 'Why is that out of the ordinary?'

'The military never charter civilian aircraft, for obvious security reasons,' said Donny.

Mike stood up and sat on the corner of the desk. 'And medical supplies usually come into the country. There's no sense in sending them back out.'

Jack nodded. 'Right. What about flight plan information?'

Mike looked at the document again. 'Says Bahrain.'

Donny stood up. 'Contact our guys in Bahrain. See if they have that flight arriving?'

Mike opened the office door. 'Stacy, can you get onto Bahrain Operations, please. I need to speak to the General Manager.'

A couple of minutes later the phone rang. 'Hello? Yeah, hi, this is Mike Sanderson in Kabul.'

Jack and Donny listened as pleasantries were exchanged and questions asked. Mike hung up the phone and turned to the two men. 'No aircraft with that call sign or cargo has ever arrived in Bahrain.'

'Looks like a dead-end, Jack,' said Donny.

Jack was already on his smartphone, scrolling through Charlie Webster's documents. 'Maybe not. I have info here about an aircraft leaving Kabul on the date in question. It's listed as a VIP flight, destined for a location in Southern Russia. It mentions a place called Kamenka.'

Donny looked at Jack. 'So, we know a suspect flight left Kabul, but did not land in Bahrain. Your info says a flight ex Kabul was destined for Russia. It's got to be the same one, Jack. Looks like you have your confirmation.'

'Hold on guys,' said Mike, 'what was on this bloody plane? Obviously not medical supplies.'

Jack looked at Mike. 'Might be best you don't know, buddy.'

It was late afternoon when Jack and Donny got back to their Bagram accommodation. They'd chatted about the information Mike had provided and how it all correlated with Charlie Webster's documents. Back in Donny's office Jack had tried to call his father in law, Dimitri Orlov, but with no success.

Dimitri Mikhailovich Orlov, was a billionaire Russian oligarch. He had interests in oil, mining and steel, as well as a large portfolio of properties in London and New York. He owned a major football club in the north of England and a prestigious golf club in Scotland. He also had contacts from New York to Japan; mostly though, he had many loyal friends in the former KGB.

Jack tried the call again and nodded to Donny as the connection was made. 'Hello, Mitri. How are you, sir?'

45

'Jack, Hello my boy, I'm good, everything okay, family alright?'

'Yes, sir, all good. Nicole and the girls are fine. I'm hoping you can help me with some information, please?'

'Of course. Tell me?'

'Have you ever heard of an airbase or airfield called Kamenka? It's in Southern Russia.'

'Not sure I have, Jack. But I can find out. When do you need the information?'

'I know your always busy, Mitri, but soon as possible, please.'

'Okay, I'll call you when I have something. Anything else?'

'That's it for now, sir.'

'Right, talk soon, Jack, bye.'

'Thanks, Mitri.'

Almost an hour had passed when Jack's phone beeped. 'Hello again, Mitri.'

'Jack, sorry to take so long, I had to take a couple of other calls.'

'No problem, sir.'

'Right, Kamenka is an old abandoned KGB airfield, just outside Volgograd. It's been shut down since the end of the Cold War. But my source tells me it's used from time to time by the Moscow Mafia, to bring in drugs from South American and Asia.'

There was silence on the line. 'Jack? You still there, Jack?'

'Sorry Mitri. That's excellent information, sir. Ties in with my investigation.'

'Investigation? What you up to, Jack?'

46

'Can't really say on an open line.'

'Okay, I understand. Be careful, my boy, you have a family to think of now.'

'Of course, sir. Thanks again for the help. Bye for now.'

'Bye, Jack. Be safe.'

Jack opened the small fridge and took out a can of Red Bull.

Donny looked impatient. 'Well? What did he say?'

'It's an old abandoned KGB airstrip, now used by the bloody Mafia.'

'Jesus, mate. You sure you know what you're doing?'

Jack finished his Red Bull and inadvertently burped. 'Oh, scuse me, sorry. Yeah I'm sure.'

'So what's your plan?'

Jack crushed the can and dropped it into the waste basket. 'Can you get your guys to book me on the next available flight to Moscow, please, buddy?'

Chapter Nine
'The Stallion'

On the outskirts of Houston, retired Colonel Jasper
Mickelson sipped his morning coffee as he read the
Chronicle. He'd slept fitfully, after hearing another of his
old comrades had died *accidentally*. A widower,
Mickelson now ran a profitable ranch and stud farm with
his two sons. His thoughts were interrupted by his eldest
son Randy. 'Morning, Dad.'

'Good morning, son, where's your brother?'

'Traye is loading the stallion, sir. Soon as you finish
your coffee, we can get movin.'

The colonel dropped the newspaper into the trash bin
as he walked to the door. 'I'm ready let's go.'
Outside in the main yard, Traye Mickelson was having a
problem with the loading of the big animal. The skittish
thoroughbred reared up, stomped its hooves and kicked
up a sizeable dust cloud in its effort to stay out of the
horse-box. His older brother ran across and took hold of
the frightened animal's bridle, pulling hard down. Then,
as he looked the magnificent creature in the eyes, he
spoke quietly, calming the stallion then gently coaxed
the big horse up the ramp and into the back of the trailer.
He secured the bridle straps to the sides of the box and,
as he came down the ramp smiled at Traye. 'Sometimes
you gotta treat em like women, bro. A firm hand, eye
contact and gentleness. Works every time.'

The colonel laughed. 'Close him up boys, the big
fella's got a date with a cute mare over

48

at McCloud's today.'

The Mickelsons had been driving for about thirty minutes when they left the highway and turned onto the private road to the McCloud Ranch. Randy had noticed the big 4x4 in the rear mirror several miles back but it was only after it turned off and followed them onto the ranch road that he spoke. 'We got a crazy guy behind us, flashing his lights.'

The colonel looked in the side mirror. 'Slow down, son, let the idiot pass.'

The following morning the lead story in the Houston Chronicle was of a retired army colonel and his two sons who'd been killed during the theft of a valuable stallion. The newspaper reported how the trailer was found empty, while the bullet riddled vehicle had the bodies of Colonel Jasper Mickelson and his sons Randy and Traye. The local police said they were doing all possible to find the perpetrators of this terrible crime.

* * *

In the back of his limo, President Elect Alex Mason was on his way to the Senate when his smartphone signalled an incoming message. He swiped the screen and the message appeared showing the Houston Chronicle's piece about the robbery and killing on the McCloud road. Mason smiled as he took out a fine leather cigar wallet. He carefully removed a Monte Christo and ran the expensive cigar under his nostrils as he savoured the delicate aroma. Pressing the intercom he said to the driver. 'Go through the park please, Henry. I'm in no rush today.'

* * *

It would be over a month until the rotting, half eaten carcass of the thoroughbred would be found by an old Cherokee Indian walking his dog.

Chapter Ten
'The Undertaker'

In Afghanistan, Jack and Donny had made an early start and by four-thirty they'd eaten breakfast and were on their way to Kabul International Airport. As usual the airport was packed with locals and expats. Donny had helped with the laborious security procedures by flashing various high level ID badges and by six-thirty he waved his old friend through the gate to Departures.

The Business Class lounge was marginally better than waiting in the main area and, although busy, Jack managed to get a mug of tea and a suspect Danish. After checking for a signal on his smartphone he hit the speed-dial for home.

On the side table, Nicole's phone beeped. She quickly shuffled across the big bed. 'Zaikin?'
    'Hi, darling. Did I wake you?'
    'No. Are you okay?'
    'I'm fine, Nikki. How're the girls?'
    'We're all good. Nice to hear your voice. Where are you, Jack?'
    'I'm leaving Kabul shortly. Got a flight to Istanbul and then on to Moscow this afternoon.'
    Nicole sat up in bed. 'Moscow?'
    'Yeah. What you up to today, baby?'

She looked at the clock. 'I'm going into the office for an hour or two, then taking the girls to the village fete this afternoon.'

'Sounds fun, sorry I'm missing it.'

'Don't worry, darling.'

'Okay, baby, will call you from Moscow. I love you.'

'Take care, Zaikin. Love you.'

He heard the sound of a kiss, and smiled.

Jack's flight was over an hour late departing Afghanistan but as he had a good two hours to wait in Istanbul, there would be no problem with his Aeroflot connection to Moscow. The Business Class cabin was full and he was surprised Donny's guy had even managed to get him a seat at such short notice. Jack found himself seated next to an attractive Russian thirty-something, who was very keen to engage him in conversation from the moment he loaded his bag into the overhead locker. She introduced herself as Irina and said she was a model. Jack was polite and charming and, at any other time, would have enjoyed passing away the flight in the company of a nice looking woman, but today he had no desire to spend the next two and a half hours chit-chatting. The initial conversation faded, along with her perfect smile, when he told her he was an undertaker.

The plane landed ahead of schedule into Domodedovo Airport and, after a few pleasantries to the model, Jack made his way as fast as possible through Immigration, Customs and the exit. The taxi rank was busy but the queue moved quickly and, just over an hour after leaving the airport, he walked into the elegant reception area of the Metropolitan Hotel. He handed his passport to the pretty receptionist along with a credit card. 'Good afternoon, Jack Castle, checking in. I've booked a suite.'

The girl looked up from the computer. 'Yes of course. Nice to have you back again, Mr Castle.'

The girl returned his documents, then waved to a smartly dressed bell-boy who came forward to pick up Jack's bag.

'It's okay, son,' said Jack, 'I know the way. Thanks.'

The sitting room looked out over the Moscow Canal and across the river to the Kremlin and St Basils. Standing by the window, he made a quick call to Nicole and then to his brother Mathew.

'Hello, Jack. You okay?'

'Hi, Matt. Yeah fine. I'm in Moscow.'

'How were things in Afghanistan? You didn't get caught up in the bombings?'

'We were close but got away without any problem.'

'That's good. Anything else you can talk about now?'

'Yeah, the package we are auditing definitely left Kabul and went to Southern Russia. I have some good intel and that's why I'm here.'

'Okay good. Do you need anything from me?'

'Not at the moment. I'll be in touch soon. Cheers, bro.'

'Just a second, Jack. One more thing.'

Jack frowned, 'What is it?

'Two more members on your list that have resigned. One from Texas and one in Virginia.'

The phone was silent. 'Jack? You still there?' said Mathew.'

'Yes, I'm here. Okay, Matt, we need to move faster. I'll be in touch.'

'You be careful, Jack, Bye for now.'

Chapter Eleven
'Grigory'

Before he left Kabul, Jack had tried to contact his old friend Bogdan Markov. He had two numbers for the Russian, his cellphone and his home, but there had been no response from either number. He'd left two voicemails and sent two texts, again none of which had been answered.

Bogdan Markov in his younger days had been a helicopter pilot with the Spetznaz, the Russian Special Forces. Jack had first met him in Kosovo after the Russian had left the Soviet military. Bogdan was working as a mercenary and secured himself a lucrative contract as a mountain guide working for the United Nations. Markov had been seconded to a mission Jack had been given to neutralise a particularly nasty Armenian warlord. It was on that mission a mutual respect and friendship had developed. Jack had last seen Bogdan over a year ago, when they'd worked together on the *Beirut Shahadi* operation. Now and for the last few years, his old friend had been working with the Moscow Mafia. Bogan also owned and operated the trendy and exclusive night club in the Metropolitan Hotel.

After eating dinner in the hotel's elegant dining room, Jack walked across the Moskvoretski Bridge and up into

Red Square. The evening was warm and the square was packed with tourists and street vendors touting for their business. He walked past St Basils and the Lenin Monument and out the other side onto Varvarka Street. Turning right, he continued past the imposing Bolshoi Theatre and then left into a small side road.

The Anna Karenina was a small but stylish café in the theatre district. The place was busy with pre-show diners but the bar area was reasonably quiet. Jack took a seat at the end of the counter and ordered a Coke. The pretty girl behind the bar smiled when he thanked her in Russian, his English accent still discernible. He handed her a twenty dollar bill and said, 'Keep the change, love.'

The pretty smile widened.

'I'm looking for a friend of mine,' said Jack.

The smile disappeared and her dark eyes narrowed.

'Is Grigory here tonight?' he smiled and waited for the girl to answer.

'Mr Markov will be here about nine o'clock, sir.'

'Okay, thanks. What's your name?'

The smile appeared again. 'Larissa.'

Jacked checked his Rolex and then looked at the girl. 'Thanks, Larissa, '

Forty five minutes later, Grigory Markov entered the café. Jack had never met the man before but there was no mistaking the likeness between him and his brother

56

Bogdan. The big man smiled and nodded to the patrons as he made his way slowly to the bar. Jack watched as the girl leaned forward and whispered to the big Russian. He nodded and smiled at her, then turned away and spoke to another couple of diners before making his way towards Jack.

'You are looking for Grigory Markov, Englishman?'

Jack stood up and smiled at the slight insult. He offered his hand and said, 'I'm an old friend of your brother Bogdan's. My name is Jack Castle.'

The Russian took Jack's hand and grinned. 'Jack Castle. I have heard of you many times from Bogdan. You are welcome my friend. How did you know to find me here?'

'Bogdan told me you owned this place. He always said if I ever needed help in Moscow to contact him. But if he was not here, then you were the next best thing.'

'And of course you have not been able to contact him, Mr Jack.'

'Just call me Jack, Grigory. That's right I've tried. I asked the manager of Bogdan's night club in the hotel but he was very tight lipped.'

'Yes, he would be, how you say, tight lipped,' the Russian grinned. 'But I am keeping eye on club while my brother is away.'

'Away where?'

'Bogdan is in prison, Jack.'

Chapter Twelve
'Lubyanka'

It was after midnight when Jack got back to the Metropolitan. Grigory wanted to hear all the stories first hand that Bodgan had told about Jack Castle and although Jack hadn't wanted to spend as long in the café, it would have been an insult to leave. It was clear, when he eventually did manage to say goodnight, he'd made another friend in Grigory Markov. Back in his suite he called his brother Mathew.

'Hello, Jack. Everything okay?'

'Yes, kind of. I'm here in Moscow and need to speak to my old friend Bogdan. Problem is he's in prison.'

'That's a big ask, Jack. We couldn't possibly get him out.'

Jack laughed. 'No of course not, you idiot. But you can get me in to talk to him.'

'Not sure we could do that either. It'd have to be through our Moscow Embassy and it would look very strange someone from our side wanting to talk to a convicted Russian felon. Even if he is your pal.'

'Yeah I guess so. Not to worry, I'll sort it out.'

'Anything else?'

'No, that's it for now. I'll be in touch after I've spoken with Bogdan.'

'Okay. Night, bro. You be safe.'

'Cheers, Matt.' Jack looked at his Rolex. It was almost two-thirty in the morning in the Emirates but he made the call anyway.

'Jack, hello. Everything alright, my boy?'

'Dimitri, I'm so sorry to wake you but I need a little more help please?'

'It's fine, Jack. I'm not in the Emirates, I'm in Tokyo. What can I do for you?'

'I urgently need to get to talk to someone in Lubyanka Prison.'

'What's his name?'

'Bogdan Markov.'

'Okay, I'll see what I can do. Talk soon.'

'Thanks, Mitri.'

Jack had fallen asleep watching TV and was startled awake when his phone beeped a few minutes before two-o'clock. 'Mitri, hello.'

'Have you a pen, Jack?'

'Just a second . . . Okay, go ahead.'

'Senior Officer Micha Kolkin will be at the main gate, at ten in the morning. He'll escort you in and you will have fifteen minutes with your man.'

'That's great. Thank you again, Mitri.'

'I hope you know what you're doing, Jack. I do worry about you sometimes. You be careful.'

Jack gave a little chuckle. 'Of course, sir. I will. Thanks again.'

The baroque building in Moscow's Lubyanka Square, which now bears the same name, was originally built for the All Russian Insurance Company. After the Revolution, the huge building was seized by the Communist Government and became the home of the KGB, now known as the Federal Security Service, or

FSB. Although the building's main purpose was and is the headquarters of the secret police, the massive basements and subterranean areas were, and still are, used as a short term correctional facility.

It had started to rain as the taxi pulled up at the main gate of the prison. The cab driver had not spoken to Jack from the moment he'd been asked to go to Lubyanka; instead the old Russian had constantly eyed up the foreigner in the rear view mirror. Not even after Jack tipped him a twenty did the suspicious look change on the old man's face.

Jack checked the time, nine-fifty-five, then walked up to the solid steel doors. The Cyrillic sign above the brass bell push translated as, PRESS FOR ATTENTION.

The small access door in the big gate creaked open and a smartly uniformed guard waved him through. In his best Russian, Jack smiled and said, 'Good Morning. I'm Jack Castle. I'm here to meet Senior Officer Kolkin.'

The guard indicated a small building to the side of the gate and Jack entered.

'Mister Castle? I'm Kolkin.'

Jack offered his hand but there was no handshake. 'You have powerful friends, Mister Castle.'

'I'm sorry to inconvenience you, sir.'

'No inconvenience for me. Please give your passport to the guard and sign the book.'

Jack did as he'd been asked, after which the guard clipped a plastic visitors badge onto Jack's lapel. Kolkin made a slight grunting sound and said, 'This way, please.'

After several minutes of walking through unwelcoming corridors and locked gates, Jack was shown into a small, dimly lit room, with a metal table and two chairs. Sitting on one of the chairs was Bogdan Markov.

Bogdan stood, arms open, as Jack moved towards him.

'No contact,' barked Kolkin. Please take your seats.' The officer looked at his watch, 'You have fifteen minutes,' then turned, grunted, and left the room.

Jack smiled, leaned forward, and spoke quietly in English. 'Good to see you, my friend.'

'You too, boss. You here to get me out?'

'Wish I could, buddy.'

'Is not problem. Only two more months in this shit hole. Is easy.'

'I spoke with your brother Grigory last night. He told me all about your problem with the police trying to extort from you.'

'Da, these stupid bastards come to my club and want money. I give them broken faces. So I am here for six months.'

Jack grinned. 'A little holiday then, eh?'

The big Russian smiled. 'Da, just holiday. Okay, boss. We have little time. What do you need?'

After leaving Lubyanka, Jack spent the rest of the day walking around the city. By late afternoon he was back at the hotel. He checked emails and messages and made a call to Nicole. Before dinner he took a swim and then spent over an hour in the sauna, only leaving when an over amorous young couple made him feel like a gooseberry, having declined the couple's offer to join in; he left them to their fun. By eleven-thirty he was back in his suite and sound asleep.

Chapter Thirteen
'Friend or Foe'

The Spanish sun was hot, but the breeze coming down from the mountain behind the villa made the afternoon bearable. Jack watched Nicole swimming, tanned arms and legs working in unison as she glided from one side of the infinity pool to the other. She moved to the steps and he watched as she emerged bare breasted. She walked sensuously to his lounger and bent down to kiss him . . .

The thud next to his head startled him awake. In one swift movement he threw off the duvet and was out of bed as the lights came on. In the corner of the room sat a smartly dressed man holding a silenced Tokarev automatic, a thin wisp of smoke drifted from the muzzle of the gun, the smell of cordite permeated the air. He was flanked by two younger, very fit looking men.

'What the hell is this?'

'Please. Mr Castle, stay calm and all will be well,' said the man.

'Who are you and what do you want?'

'All in good time,' smiled the gunman. He looked at Jack standing there naked and continued. 'My name is Drogan. You are in pretty good shape for your age, Mr Castle.'

The taller of the two young men smiled.

'What? You're here because you fancy me or something?'

The tall henchman lost his grin and made to move towards Jack, fist clenched. The older man held up his hand and the henchman resumed his position.

'Neat trick,' said Jack, 'can you get him to roll over?'

Drogan lowered the gun from Jack's chest to his groin. 'Choose your next witticism carefully, Mr Castle, it may be your last.'

'Okay, what do you want?'

'I think we'll start by you getting dressed and then we are going to take a little drive.'

'I'm not fucking going anywhere with you.'

'Please. Mr Castle, if we wanted to kill you, you would not be standing there now. So please get dressed.'

Several minutes later Jack and the three Russians climbed into a gleaming black Range Rover. Through the dark tinted windows Jack could see an identical vehicle, its engine running, behind them. In the back seat one of the henchmen grinned and handed Jack a white hood.

'Really?' said Jack, 'is this necessary?'

'Please. Mr Castle, indulge us,' said Drogan.

Jack slipped the hood over his head and through the thick material said, 'Well at least you are the politest guys I've ever been kidnapped by.'

Almost an hour and a half later the vehicles came to a stop. Jack was manhandled out of his seat and the sweat soaked hood removed from his head. He blinked at the bright sunlight, rubbed his eyes and ran his fingers through his hair.

Drogan smiled. 'I must apologise for all the secrecy, Mr Castle but not many people know of this place.'

Jack looked at the imposing building in front of him, all it needed was Omar Sharif and Julie Christie on the steps and it would have been a scene right out of *Doctor Zhivago*. The immediate area surrounding the building was resplendent with beautifully cultivated gardens and mature trees but beyond that and as far as the eye could see, was nothing but open fields. This place was, to say the least, remote.

The taller of the two henchmen pushed Jack towards the steps. Drogan turned and swore at him, then looked at Jack. 'Please excuse my colleague. This way, Mr Castle.'

The four men entered the house and were greeted by an attractive Russian woman. Drogan leaned in close and spoke quietly in her ear, then turned to Jack. 'I will see you later, Mr Castle.'

The woman smiled and said in perfect English, 'This way please, sir.'

Jack followed the woman to the rear of the house and out through the large patio doors. In the elegant garden an old man was seated, eating breakfast. A heavy set, tough looking guy stood away to the side.

'This is, Mr Castle, sir,' said the woman.

The old man smiled and nodded. 'Thank you, Elena,' then looked at Jack and pointed to a chair. 'Please have a seat.'

Jack sat down and looked the old man straight in the eye. 'Why am I here?'

The man wiped his mouth with his napkin and held Jack's gaze. 'You have been asking questions about my business, Jack. May I call you, Jack?'

'Yeah sure, what do I call you?'

'Let's leave that for the moment and chat a while. Would you like some breakfast?'

Jack shook his head slightly. 'No. Let's just get on with it.'

The old man was about to speak when a younger man joined them, leaned down and kissed the old man's cheek. 'Good morning, father.'

'Good morning, Vanya. This is Mr Castle. He is the Englishman who has been so very interested in our business with the Americans.'

'Jack, this is my son, Vanya and he tells me you are a relative of Dimitri Mikhailovich Orlov?'

Suddenly Jack felt relaxed at the mention of his father-in-law's name. 'You know Dimitri?'

A wry smile appeared on the old man's lips. 'Oh yes, I know him very well.'

'Then you will know Dimitri has many powerful friends in Russia?'

'Yes indeed.' The old man raised his head and traced his finger along a thick white scar that ran from below his left ear, to the right side of his chin. 'He also has powerful enemies, Jack. He gave me this many years ago. I still have to return the favour. And now I have his daughter's husband.'

Jack leaned back in his chair. 'So you're going to kill me to get back at Dimitri?'

'Maybe, I haven't made my mind up yet?'

66

'If you wanted to kill me, you would have done so at my hotel. Your man Drogan said as much. So what do you want? And am I going to get to know who I'm being held by?'

The old Russian smiled and took a sip of tea. 'My name is Alexei Kuragin.'

Jack looked at the man in front of him and was about to speak, when Kuragin said, 'I see from the look on your face that name means something to you, Jack. You have heard of me?'

Jack smiled for the first time that morning. 'I've heard of you, Mr Kuragin and of your son. I also know you are a man of honour; ruthless but still a man of honour.'

Alexei leaned forward. 'And why do you say this, Jack?'

'Because a man of honour, especially a man with your reputation and position, would always honour his debts.'

'And what debt do you speak of?'

The smile on Jack's face widened. 'Bogdan Markov. And I think I will have some breakfast after all.'

In the end, the meeting with Alexie Kuragin could not have gone better.

It had been over a year earlier when Bogdan told Jack the story of how he'd been recruited into the mafia family, after saving the life of the old boss's son. It only took a few minutes for a phone call to be made to Lubyanka Prison and, via various guards on their payroll; Vanya Kuragin had spoken directly with Bogdan Markov. With a confirmation that Jack Castle

67

was indeed a very old and close friend of Bogdan's, the threat of anything untoward happening was negated and Jack, even though being related to Dimitri Orlov, was treated as a friend.

Jack had taken Alexie Kuragin into his confidence. He explained he was not the least bit interested in any business the Kuragin family were involved in and that his only goal was to see President Elect Alex Mason, brought to justice. After Jack had told the old boss Mason was killing off everyone involved with the Bagram heist, Kuragin had opened up in a big way. The meeting had finished with handshakes and entreaties of future possible cooperation, should Jack ever need it in Russia.

On the front steps of the fine old house, Alexie and Vanya Kuragin said goodbye and apologised for the continued use of the blindfold. Jack climbed into the back of the Range Rover and nodded to the two men, just before the white hood was once again placed over his head.

Chapter Fourteen
'You Hear That?'

In the Arctic Ocean, one hundred and fifty miles north of Murmansk, the American nuclear submarine, USS Endeavour, broke the surface. The cloudless black sky was studded with stars and the light from an almost full moon shimmered on the wet deck of the long sleek vessel.

The large cargo hatch directly behind the conning-tower hissed open and the elevator rose to the deck. On the platform stood one of the latest long-range Unmanned Ariel Vehicles, more commonly referred to as a drone. The sea-swell was minimum and the waves around the sub lapped lazily against the steel hull. The quiet of the night was fractured by the sound of the compact jet engine being fired-up, then, as the noise increased, a flame shot from the afterburner and the small aircraft raced along the spine of the submarine. As the drone cleared the deck and lifted into the night sky, the cargo hatched hissed shut and the Endeavour slipped below the cold black waters of the Arctic.

* * *

In his dacha north of Moscow, Alexei Kuragin looked at the ceiling above the bed, his thoughts still on the meeting with the Englishman earlier that day. His mistress stirred and then turned to face him. She moved in close and stroked his chest. 'Darling, why don't you sleep?'

'Shhh, Marina. I'm fine, go back to sleep.'

She moved closer still and pressed her warm body against his. He murmured as she smiled and eased herself onto him. The strange humming sound distracted him and he pushed her off. 'Do you hear that?'

They were the last words either of them ever heard.

* * *

The following morning, Jack had agreed to Grigory's offer of a lift out to the airport. It was still raining when the big Mercedes pulled up under the portico of the Metropolitan Hotel. Jack was waiting on the steps as the blacked-out window was lowered and Grigory Markov leaned out and waved him in. As they drove away the big Russian smiled. 'Good morning.'

'Good morning, Grigory. You didn't have to do this.'

'Is fine. I like to drive.' The big smile remained. 'So you managed to get in to see Bogdan, da?'

'Yeah, I did. He's okay. He sends his regards. He also asked me to tell you to make sure all the takings from his night club go into the safe.'

The big Russian laughed out loud. 'He is cheeky bastard.'

'And you, Grigory? Your business is well?'

'Da, da, business is good.' The smile disappeared. 'But I think there is much trouble to come now.'

Jack turned to his new friend. 'Why is that?'

'There is word on street. We don't know for sure yet. But people say Alexie Kuragin was killed last night. He

70

has secret house north of Moscow. They say house was totally destroyed.'

Chapter Fifteen
'Mathew's Office'

The Business Class cabin was almost full, mostly with Russians but Jack nodded and spoke to a couple of British business men as he loaded his bag into the locker. Once seated, he made a quick call to Nicole to let her know he would be home later that day. His next call was to his brother Mathew.

The Aeroflot flight took just over three and a half hours from Moscow to Heathrow and the chauffer car had Jack at Vauxhall House a few minutes before midday. Mathew Sterling was in a meeting when Jack arrived at his outer office.

'He should be finished shortly, sir,' said the secretary, 'can I get you a drink while you wait?'

Jack smiled. 'Oh yes, I'd love some tea, please, Victoria.'

Big Ben chimed twelve-thirty as the door to Mathew's office opened. Jack nodded to a couple of smartly dressed men as Victoria showed them out. She turned quickly. 'You can go in now, sir.' Holding the inner door open she said, 'Mr Castle, sir.'

'Jack, come in,' said Mathew. 'Thank you, Victoria. Can I have some tea please? You want some, Jack?'

Jack shook his head. 'Just had some, thanks,' then sat down in front of the big desk.

After the door closed, Mathew looked at his brother. 'You look tired.'

'I'm okay, sorry to barge in on you.'

72

'Not a problem. So what else do we have on our friend Mason?'

'Right. I managed to get into Lubyanka to see Bogdan. He confirmed the Moscow Mafia took delivery of the opium back in two thousand and three.'

A knock on the door interrupted the conversation.

'Come in.'

Victoria put the tray down on the corner of his desk. Mathew smiled. 'Thank you, Victoria. No calls for now, please.'

'Of course, sir.'

'Go on, Jack,' said Mathew.

'Bogdan told me as much as he could in the short time we had, which was good as it corroborated the info we had about the old KGB airfield at Kamenka.'

'Still doesn't prove the Mafia actually took delivery, Jack. No offence intended but it's just the word of a dodgy Russian.'

Jack grinned. 'He's that alright. But he's solid when it comes to friendship and would definitely not bullshit me.'

Mathew stood up and poured a cup of tea. 'Still doesn't prove anything, though.'

'Ah, well, there's more.'

'Go on.'

'I got a visit from the mob during the night. They took me from my suite and drove me out to a secret location, north of Moscow.'

'Secret?'

'I was hooded, so I've no idea where it was. It was about a ninety-minute drive out of the city. But I'll get to that in a second.'

'Sorry, go on,' said Mathew.

'So I get to meet the boss and it turns out it's the guy Bogdan works for, Alexei Kuragin.'

'Bogdan saved his son's life, yeah?'

'That's right. The very same. So we're all pals now and when I tell him we're not interested in his business, we're after that bastard Mason, he opens up.'

'Really? They're usually pretty tight lipped when it comes to their business dealings.'

'Of course they are. But when I told him Mason was killing off everyone who was involved, he was happy to chat.'

'But Alexei Kuragin was not on Charlie Webster's list?'

'I know and I'll get to that in a second. Kuragin confirmed a deal was done with an American colonel called Mickelson.'

Mathew stood up and went to the window. 'He's one of the men who were killed a few days ago.'

'Right.' Jack stood up and joined his brother at the window. 'So Kuragin tells me they paid almost one billion dollars for the cargo. Six hundred thousand was paid into several bank accounts in the Caymans. The rest was paid in diamonds and smuggled into the States, through Alaska and Canada.'

Mathew shook his head. 'Jesus, Jack, these fuckers don't mess about.'

'You haven't heard the best part.' Jack took out his smartphone and spent several seconds swiping the screen and then passed it to his brother. 'Take a look at this.'

Mathew put on his glasses and slowly scrolled through the files. 'These are the bank accounts in the Caymans.'

'That's right. You'd better down load them now. Keep them safe.'

'This is fantastic, Jack. Anything else?'

'Yeah, one last thing. Grigory Markov, Bogdan's brother, drove me out to the airport this morning. He told me the word on the street is Alexei Kuragin was killed last night. Apparently the whole house was destroyed. I was in that house and it was huge. It would've needed a lot of explosive to destroy the place.'

Mathew sat down at his desk. 'Or a missile?'

Chapter Sixteen
'Good to be Home'

The prison communal shower area was dimly lit, hot and steamy. Windowless, with broken tiled walls and floor, the facility was unpleasant to say the least. The pungent smell emanating from the antiquated drainage system made this place somewhere you used and got out fast. Not only were the showers unwelcoming but the likelihood of being assaulted, raped, or worse, made the inmates very cautious of lingering in the area alone. Hence the reason daily ablutions were usually taken en-mass.

A dozen naked men shouted, swore and cajoled each other as they indulged in their communal cleansing. Although body shapes and sizes were varied, one thing was constant; every man was heavily embellished with religious, ornate and ritualistic tattoos.

Bogdan Markov, eyes closed, face turned to the overhead spray, heard the shouts above his fellow inmates clamour.

'Everybody out. Now.'

After wiping the water from his eyes and face, Markov turned to see three burly guards standing in the centre of the shower area, unusually dressed in riot body armour, helmets and heavy batons. The guards continued to yell at the naked men as they hurried to leave the area. Bogdan turned off the shower and took his towel from the peg, wrapped it around his waist and made for the exit.

'Not you, asshole.'

* * *

Jack had left Mathew's office a little after one o'clock. It had just started to rain but it was only a few minutes' walk to the Underground. He took the tube from Embankment to Paddington and after jogging to the platform managed to catch the overland train out to Berkshire. He arrived at East Monkton a few minutes before two-thirty. The rain had stopped and the sun was pushing its way through the watery clouds as Nicole pulled up in front of the little station. Jack nodded to the attendant as he hurriedly made his way to the waiting car. He opened the rear door and threw in his bag, then climbed into the front seat.

As he leaned across to kiss her he said, 'Hi, baby.' Her perfume filled the car and the taste of her mouth on his took his breath away for a second. 'It's good to be home, darling.'

She smiled her beautiful smile and touched his cheek. 'You look tired, Zaikin.'

'I'm okay. Just need a shave and a shower. Let's get home.'

Fifteen minutes later they turned off the road and onto the drive. Jack smiled as he saw the beautiful house. 'Definitely good to be home.'

'Every time you come back you always say that.'

'Yeah, coz it's true,' said Jack.

As the 4x4 pulled up to the front door, Svetlana came out with the twins. Jack climbed out of the car and scooped up the two beautiful girls. 'Here's trouble.'

The twins wrinkled their noses as he kissed them in turn, the stubble on his face irritating their delicate cheeks.

'Welcome back, Mr Jack.'

'Thanks, Svetlana. Any chance of some tea, please?'

'Already in the drawing room, Mr Jack.'

He put the girls down and turned to collect his bag as his smartphone beeped. The display showed, GRIGORY MARKOV CALLING.

Jack swiped the screen as he walked into the house. 'Grigory, hello.'

'Priviet, hello, Jack.'

'What's up my friend? Is Bogdan okay?'

'No. Bogdan is in hospital. He is in bad way. Some broken ribs. Maybe punctured lung and maybe kidney damage'

'Fuck. What happened?'

'He was beaten in shower. Guards beat him for information.'

'What information, Grigory?'

'About you, Jack. Who you are and where you live in UK. But he tells them nothing.'

'How do you know?'

'I see him in hospital. He was pretty bad but still says he tell them nothing.'

'Who would do this, Grigory?'

'The guards did it, Jack.'

'No, I mean who would get the guards to do it? Who wants to know about me? It can't be the Americans?'

'No, not Americans. Vanya Kuragin.' The line went quiet. 'You still there Jack?'

'Yeah . . ., Yes, still here. I thought you said he was dead? That everyone was killed when the dacha was destroyed?'

'Alexie Kuragin, his mistress, three house staff and four of his men, all killed. But his son Vanya was in Moscow.' The line went quiet again . . ., 'Jack?'

'Yes, sorry. So Vanya Kuragin thinks I had something to do with his father's death?'

'Maybe. Is why he had Bogdan beaten for information.'

'Okay. Thanks for this, Grigory. Tell Bogdan I owe him one.'

'Is no problem, Jack. What you gonna do?'

'I'm going to meet Mr Vanya Kuragin and put him straight. But not just yet. I want you to set up a meeting with him. I'll let you know when and where, tomorrow.'

'Okay. Take care my friend, dasvidanya.'

Chapter Seventeen
'Bye Girls'

The VIP lounge at Heathrow was quiet but the twins running round made the place less staid.

'Are you going to tell me what's going on, Zaikin?' said Nicole.

Jack took her hand and smiled. 'Look, I told you on the way here that I have to go to America and I would rather you were not left at home alone.'

'I wouldn't be alone. Svetlana is with me.'

'Please, darling, just do as I ask for now. Your father is on his way back to Abu Dhabi already and he's delighted you and the girls are going down to Orel Island.'

'I'm fine about going to see dad and the girls will love the island but it's you I'm worried about. What's going on, Jack?'

He kissed her hand and then laughed when he turned to see Svetlana crawling under a low table after his daughters.

The attendant returned. 'Hello again, madam. Your flight is ready for departure, if your party would like to come with me, please?'

Nicole smiled at the girl. 'Okay, thank you.'

Jack stood up. 'Girls, time to go.'

The nanny recovered the twins and returned them, giggling, to Jack.

Nicole picked up her handbag and carry-on, as Svetlana collected the rest of the hand luggage.

He put his arms around her and kissed her. 'I love you, darling. Don't worry.'

She looked up into his eyes and touched his cheek. 'Please be careful. I'll call you when I get to the island.

'Okay, have a safe flight, baby. Give my regards to Dimitri.'

'Kiss daddy, girls.'

The two excited children hugged their kneeling father, then hand-in-hand with Svetlana, they followed the attendant.

Nicole kissed his cheek again. 'I love you, Zaikin. Please be careful.'

He watched as they disappeared through the exit and then turned to the big floor-to-ceiling windows. The G550 Gulfstream stood on the tarmac, its gleaming white fuselage and wings shimmering in the afternoon sun. He watched as the small minibus pulled up alongside the private jet and his family emerge. A waiting flight attendant took the hand-luggage as Svetlana helped the twins up the short flight of steps. At the open door Nicole turned, looked up to the window and blew him a kiss, then entered the cabin. The minibus pulled away and Jack continued to watch as the small flight of steps automatically retracted into the fuselage. The door closed and a second or two later he saw Nicole at one of the windows. It was a few minutes until the engines were fired up and the sleek aircraft slowly taxied away from the VIP hard-stand. The plane disappeared around the end of the terminal but he continued to wait. He saw four aircraft take off before the Gulfstream came into sight again as it accelerated down the runway. A few seconds later the nose rose and the sleek aircraft lifted off into the late afternoon sky.

Jack took a deep breath. 'Bye, girls.'

After leaving the VIP area he made his way across to Terminal 2 and the United Airways desk. He'd already checked in for the evening flight to Washington but had over three hours to wait. Instead of sitting in the Business Lounge, he took a walk round the busy terminal and ended up in one of the bars. He bought a Coke and took a seat next to the window. The sun was low in the sky now and its light streamed in through the big windows. He narrowed his eyes against the sun's rays as he sipped at the ice cold drink, his mind racing with thoughts of Bogdan, Vanya Kuragin, Alex Mason and Charlie Webster's list. His smartphone beeped and he looked at the display, MATHEW CALLING, and then swiped the screen. 'Hi, Matt. What's up?'

'Jack, hello. Did the family get off, okay?'

'Yep, they're on their way.'

'Can you talk?'

Jack looked around the busy bar. No one was paying him any attention. 'Sure, Matt. Go ahead.'

'After our chat this morning, I contacted a friend of mine at GCHQ. He's responsible for monitoring traffic from the spy satellites over Russia and Eastern Europe.'

Jack stood up and moved to the far corner of the bar area. 'Right?'

'I told him about the destruction of the Kuragin dacha and asked if he could check out anything suspicious in the region north of Moscow last night.'

'And?'

'And he got back to me a little while ago.'

'And?'

'He said they recorded a trace of a small aircraft originating in the Arctic, a couple of hundred miles north of Murmansk.'

'What? Like from an aircraft carrier?'

'That's what I said, but no. My guy tells me the aircraft was a long range drone.'

Jack looked around him again. 'But that thing would've had to take off from a ship or something?'

'Yeah, or something. My guy says the most likely platform to deploy a weapon like that would be a nuclear submarine.'

'You are fucking joking?'

'Nope. There's more. He says they have a detonation on record, approximately one fifty miles north of Moscow.' The line went quiet . . . 'Jack?'

'Yeah, I'm here. So whose sub was it?'

'Has to be the Americans. If the Russians wanted to take out the building, they'd have used a conventional aircraft. The drone is a fast-moving stealth weapon, designed specifically for covert strikes over foreign soil.'

'Jesus, Mathew, Mason's used the bloody military to rid himself of his Russian connection.'

'Looks like it, bro.'

'Right, thanks, Matt. I'll be in touch once I get to Washington.'

'Okay, Jack. Bye for now. You be safe, eh?'

Chapter Eighteen
'Lisa'

The American Airways flight took off on time. Business class was only half full, so Jack had plenty of room to spread out and relax on what was usually a boring flight. He never minded travelling to the Middle East but going the other way to the States always seemed tedious. Never-the-less, the flight of almost eight hours was comfortable, the food decent and the staff pleasant. The aircraft touched down at Dulles International a few minutes before midnight. The transfer from plane to terminal, the Immigration process and Customs check, took another hour and it was well after one in the morning when he walked out of the Arrivals Gate.

The area was packed with people waiting to meet and pick up their friends and family. Jack stood for a few seconds and scanned the waiting crowd. Then he saw her, arm raised and waving, off to the left of the melee.

He pushed through the crowd and made his way to the smiling woman standing next to one of the car-hire desks. He dropped his bag and they hugged, cheeks were kissed and more hugs followed. 'Hello, handsome.'

'Lisa . . .It's great to see you, babe. You look terrific.'

Born in New York and now almost forty, Lisa Reynard was tall and athletic; her olive skin and dark eyes were a testament to her Italian heritage. She'd become a successful and respected photo-journalist with the

Washington Post and had worked several conflict zones over the last dozen or more years. The two had originally met in Baghdad in 2003 and had become good friends. In 2008 they'd worked together on the Iraq operation to recover a vast quantity of looted diamonds; an operation that had made them both multi-millionaires. The last time Jack had worked with Lisa was over a year ago in Beirut. It was at that time Jack discovered not only was she a renowned journalist, but an agent for the NSA, the America National Security Agency.

She smiled and linked arms. 'Come on, honey. Let's get outta here.'

'Yes, please.'

'How's Nicole and your gorgeous daughters, Mr Castle?'

'All good. Nikki sends her love and wants to know when you're coming over again?'

'Oh, I'd love to but just seems to be one thing after another here.'

'They've all gone down to the island for a little while.'

She looked at him. 'I absolutely adore Orel Island. How's Dimitri?'

'As busy as ever. He was out in Japan but should be back on the island with Nikki and the girls by now.'

As they left the air-conditioned terminal, the warm night air hit them. 'The car's this way.'

The lights flashed on a Toyota Prius. 'Oh no. You've gone all save-the-planet, babe'

She laughed. 'Hybrid petro-electric cars are in, Jack, especially in big cities. You still drive your gas-guzzling Jaguar?'

He grinned. 'Always.'

She frowned and wagged her finger. 'Tut, tut, tut.' Her perfect smile returned. 'Get in.'

The drive into Washington was easy at that time of the morning, with few cars on the expressway and even less once they got into the city proper. Lisa's apartment was at the northern end of Connecticut Avenue, a couple of blocks from Rock Creek Park. She also had a beautiful country house out in West Virginia, which was used at weekends and holidays but most of her time, when working with the Post, was spent at the apartment on Connecticut.

As they entered the flat Jack looked at his Rolex. A few minutes after two, mid-morning in the Emirates. He dropped his bag; took out his smartphone and checked for a signal. 'Gonna call Nicole.'

'Okay, give her my love. Would you like some tea, honey?'

Jack walked over to the window. 'Yeah. love some, please,' then waited for the call to connect.

'Zaikin.'

'Hi, darling. You arrived okay? Girls okay?'

'We're all fine. Mike picked us up from the airport in the chopper. We're just having a late breakfast now with Dad. How about you?'

'I'm good. Just arrived at Lisa's. She sends her love.'

'Good. Say hello from me too. It's late there so I'll let you go. Call me when you can. Be careful, darling. I love you.'

Jack turned, as Lisa entered with the tea tray. 'Love you too, baby. Kiss the girls.'

'English breakfast tea, skimmed milk and sweetener,' said Lisa.

Jack flopped down on the big red Italian leather couch. 'I'm gasping for that.'

She sat down and poured his tea. 'Here you go.'

'You not having anything?'

'Not this time of night.' She leaned back against the soft leather. 'Okay, Jack. Do you want to shower and sleep? Or are you gonna tell me what this is all about?'

Chapter Nineteen
'Meet Me in Washington'

The Golden Samovar is one of Moscow's finest restaurants. Situated in the decidedly upmarket Petrovka District it is frequented by celebrities, diplomats and the wealthier element of Moscow's elite. It is also the headquarters of the Kuragin family business.

The lunch service was drawing to an end when Grigory Markov entered the elegant restaurant. The attractive girl at the desk looked him up and down. 'Good afternoon, sir. Can I help you?'

Grigory smiled and leaned a little closer. 'I have a meeting with Vanya Kuragin, I'm a few minutes early.'

'Yes, sir. May I have your name, please?'

'Markov, Grigory Markov.'

'Ah, yes sir. You can wait in the bar area.' After opening the ornate glass and ormolu doors she smiled. 'This way please, sir.'

Grigory had eaten at the Samovar several times. Being a restauranteur, he always dined in the best restaurants and although he was not as squeaky-clean as he made out, he did occasionally associate with the rather less salubrious elements in the city. That said, he was never really involved with the mafia and far less so with the Kuragin family organisation.

He remembered the night Bogdan saved the life of young Vanya. It was in his brother's night-club. The place was as busy as ever; they were at the bar with a couple of curvy blondes, when a disturbance in the VIP area got the attention of the security staff. Seeing it was at Vanya Kuragin's booth, Bogdan had gone over to ensure things were calmed down as swiftly as possible. A young man had been berating the mafia warlord's son about some woman they were both interested in. Kuragin's minders were on the verge of taking matters into their own hands when Bogdan arrived. It only took a few minutes of calm talking and the promise of Champagne and girls and the irate interloper was ready to leave. The man had calmed down and was walking away from the booth when a slur on his birth-right by Kuragin caused him to turn. Pride and foolhardiness got the better of him and he pulled a gun from the back of his waistband and fired at the seated Vanya. It was only the swift actions of Bogdan that saved Kuragin's life, the bullet hitting Bogdan in the shoulder instead of Vanya's head.

From that day on, the Kuragin family and especially the old boss, had been beholden to Grigory's brother. Of course when the dacha north of Moscow had been destroyed and his father killed, all bets were off, and the crazed Vanya was now looking for revenge on everyone involved.

The Louis Quatorze clock behind the bar chimed three as Vanya Kuragin and two other men entered. Grigory swallowed his third vodka and stood up. The look on Vanya Kuragin's face was not welcoming. 'You are, Markov? Bogdan's brother?'

'Yes, I am Markov.'

'You have information on the murder of my father?'

'I believe so.'

Kuragin turned and walked towards the back of the restaurant. Grigory followed, the two henchmen brought up the rear. Vanya Kuragin stopped in front of an ornate but solid looking door. He tapped out a code on the keypad and the door clicked opened to a small foyer at the bottom of a steep set of stairs. At the top they walked along a tastefully decorated corridor and into a large office. Kuragin sat down at a beautiful old carved desk that allegedly had come from the Tsar's Winter Palace. Grigory stood in front of the desk, flanked by the two minders.

'So, Grigory. Tell me all you know about my father's killing.'

Grigory looked at the mafia boss, 'You had my brother beaten for information about the Englishman.'

'My father was killed the night Jack Castle came to our home.'

'And you think Jack had something to do with it?'

Vanya Kuragin's tanned face reddened with rage. 'You are here to answer my questions, not I yours.'

'Yes, of course, of course.'

Grigory moved to put his hand under his Jacket but the minders were on him.

'It's just my phone.'

One of the men reached into the pocket and removed the cellphone, then handed it to Grigory.

'May I call Jack Castle? He wishes to talk to you directly.'

Kuragin stood up, a bemused look on his face. 'He wishes to talk to me?'

'Yes,' said Bogdan.

A smile appeared on the mafia boss's face. 'Very well. Call him.'

Jack and Lisa had talked until after four-o'clock. It was now eight in the morning, as Jack emerged from the shower, his smartphone beeping on the bed. He wrapped the towel round his waist and quickly swiped the screen. 'Grigory?'

'Da, hello, Jack.'

'Are you okay?'

'Yes, I'm okay. I'm here with Mr Vanya Kuragin.'

'Well done, Grigory. Let me talk to him, please.'

Markov handed the phone to the mafia boss. 'Hello?'

'Vanya?'

'This is Vanya. You have a nerve, Jack Castle. You pretend to be a friend. You killed my father.'

Jack did not answer for several seconds and let the mafia boss vent. 'If you will listen to me I can help you.'

The tanned face reddened again. 'Go ahead.'

'We can't talk as openly as I'd like on the phone. We'll have to meet. The man responsible for your father's death is in America. I know who he is and if you meet me in Washington, I'll tell you all I know.'

'Washington? You want me to come to Washington? Do you think I'm stupid?'

'Far from it, Vanya. That is why, when you calm down and think straight, you'll meet me here.'

The line went silent for several seconds and then Kuragin said, 'Very well. When?'

'Meet me in forty eight hours from now, in front of the Lincoln Memorial.'

'Okay, I'll be there. If you are not, or of its any kind of a trap, Grigory and his brother will both be killed. Then I will come after you and you're family. Is that clear, Jack?'

'Crystal.'

There was a knock on the bedroom door. 'Yeah?' said Jack.

Lisa came in. 'Oh sorry, honey. I heard you talking. Thought you were dressed.'

Jack smiled. 'It's okay. I was just talking to Grigory and Vanya Kuragin.'

'Did he go for the meet?'

'Yep, he'll be here in forty eight hours.'

'Okay, good.' Lisa smiled, then looked at the scar across his abdomen. 'Shot in the liver, eh, Mr Castle?'

He touched the old wound. 'Yeah. A souvenir from a little job in the Arabian Gulf.'

She pulled up her T-shirt and showed a similar scar in almost the same place. 'Snap, me too. A souvenir from a little job in Moscow.'

'That's gonna spoil your bikini-look, babe.'

Lisa, frowned. 'Yeah. Full one-piece from now on,' and lowered the shirt.

Jack winked. 'Still gorgeous though.'

'Yeah right. Okay, get dressed. Breakfast's ready.'

Lisa had set breakfast out on the balcony. The rear of the apartment building looked out towards Rock Creek Park which, from the twelfth floor, could be seen over the tops of the lower buildings.

Jack sat down. 'It's nice here. Great view of the park.'

She poured the tea. 'Yeah, and being on Connecticut it's only thirty minutes into the city and forty-five to the other place.'

The 'other place' was Fort Meade, the headquarters of the National Security Service.

'Talking of the other place. You working on anything at the moment?'

'I was, but handed it off. Told my controller I had something else to look into.'

'Didn't he want to know what it was?'

'Sure, but I said I needed to work on it first. Nothing more. We don't know who's involved with our esteemed President Elect yet, do we?'

'Right, and what about your real job at the Washington Post?'

'Took some vacation, hun. I'm all yours 'til we get this job done.'

'Okay, sounds good. Now let's eat. I'm famished.'

Chapter Twenty
'Hit & Run'

There were only two people on Charlie Webster's list who were still alive; Lieutenant Colonel, Marcus Nelson and Captain Anders Bergen. They had no location for Nelson but Captain Bergen was serving with the air-force and stationed at Andrews Airforce Base.

Lisa had agreed to leave the Toyota Prius and, on Jack's insistence, took her Porsche. Jack drove and they were on their way to Maryland south east of the capitol. Although the base was only twenty minutes out of the city, it would take over an hour to get from Lisa's apartment, around the Beltway circular and down to Andrews. It was almost noon when they pulled up to the outer security gate.

'Good morning, sir. How may I help you today?'

Jack smiled at the smartly dressed air-man, noting the stripes on his arm. 'Good morning, Sergeant. We're here to see Captain Anders Bergen.'

'May I have your names, please, sir?'

'Jack Castle and Lisa Reynard.'

The sergeant looked at his clipboard and began flicking through several sheets of paper.

'We won't be on your list. We don't have an appointment.'

The air-man bent down and looked into the low vehicle, getting a smile from Lisa. 'ID's please.'

Jack handed over his passport and American Department of Defence card, Lisa passed her driving licence and Washington Post ID.

'DOD? You worked with the military in Iraq, sir?'

'Yes. My company provides security services.'

'You with the British army as well?'

'I was, but now retired.'

The sergeant nodded. 'Pull the vehicle into the holding bay please, sir. Wait in the car.'

A second air-man came out of the gate-house and stood by the Porsche. Jack watched as the sergeant went back in and made a phone call. He could see the man looking at their ID's as he spoke.

'Here we go,' said Jack, as the sergeant returned.

'Okay, sir. If you'd please come into the gate house and sign-in. We'll fix you up with a couple of Visitor's Badges.'

Sign-in formalities over the Porsche was quickly screened inside and out. And after giving precise directions to the administration building, the sergeant stood back and saluted. 'Have a good day, sir, ma'am.'

In less than a minute they pulled into a visitor parking bay in front of the admin block. As they left the car a young officer came out of the building. 'Mr Castle? Miss Reynard?'

'Yes, sir,' said Jack, offering his hand.

'This way, please,' said the officer.

They followed the man into a small foyer and then along a bright corridor with several rooms leading off. At the end was an empty lounge area.

'Please have a seat. Can I get you anything? Water?'

Jack shook his head slightly. 'Nothing for me.'

'I'm fine,' smiled Lisa.'

'Captain Bergen is my senior officer. May I ask what business you have with him, sir?'

'Lisa and I were in Afghanistan several years ago. We met and became friends with Anders, Captain Bergen, over there. I'm in DC on business for a few days and we thought we might all get together. Our business is purely personal I'm afraid.'

The young officer frowned. 'I see. I'm sorry to have to tell you, sir, but Captain Bergen was in an accident in town last night. He was hit by a car. A hit and run actually.'

Jack looked at Lisa, then at the officer. 'Is he dead?'

'No, sir. But he sustained serious injuries and a critical head trauma. He's very ill.'

Lisa leaned forward. 'Is he here in the base hospital?'

'No ma'am. They took him to Walter Reed Military Hospital.'

Jack stood up. 'That's dreadful news.'

The officer stood. 'Yes indeed. I'm sorry, sir.'

'Okay, thank you, Lieutenant,' said Jack. 'I guess we'll get out of your hair.'

Back in the car they waved to the officer and made their way back to the gate. The sergeant appeared and handed back their documents, retrieving the visitor's cards.

Jack nodded and smiled. 'Thanks again.'

The sergeant saluted. 'Good afternoon, sir, ma'am. Have a good day.'

As they drove through the gate Jack turned to Lisa. 'Which way to the hospital?'

Chapter Twenty One
'The Doctor'

The Beltway was a lot busier on the return journey and it took well over an hour to travel north to the hospital. The Walter Reed Medical facility is vast and set in its own grounds in the Bethesda district of Washington. Parking for civilian vehicles is provided below ground, under the main administration building and consists of five levels, each with spaces for over three hundred vehicles. Jack had to drive to the lowest level before they found a vacant space.

They left the car and took one of the four elevators up to ground level and out into the main reception foyer. Several receptionists manned the large enquires counter and after persuading one of them Lisa was Anders Bergen's fiancé, they managed to gain access to the intensive care unit where Bergen was being treated.

The stern looking ward sister was not happy about her patient having visitors but, when Lisa broke down in tears, the tough nurse's demeanour softened and directions were given to the captain's private side ward.

'This is it,' said Lisa, as she pointed to a door a few yards away.

The door opened and a doctor came out, smiling as he passed them.

Jack stopped and turned to look at the retreating doctor, Lisa opened the door and they entered. The room was well lit with the afternoon sun streaming in on the sleeping man's face. Several machines were sited around the bed, each with cables or tubes attached to Bergen's body. Lisa moved to the bedside, as Jack said, 'Look . . . the machines are all switched off.'

She felt the captain's pulse and turned to Jack. 'He's dead.'

'Tell the nurse. I'm going after that doctor!'

As Jack ran along the corridor he almost knocked the stern ward sister off her feet, her shouts echoed in his ear as he turned the corner, just in time to see the lift doors closing.

He hit the button several times then turned and ran for the emergency stairwell, almost knocking over another nurse as he burst through the heavy door. He was on the third flight down when he heard Lisa shouting, her footsteps clattering on the concrete steps above him. Two more flights and he was out and into the first level sub parking area. He quickly looked around and saw no movement anywhere. *Where was the bastard? No spaces here, the fifth level had space!* His brain racing, he ran back into the stairwell knocking Lisa over and shouting, 'Lowest level.'

A few seconds later they crashed through the emergency door and into the parking area.

'Over there.' Lisa's raised hand pointed to a white van parked in the corner. 'The doctor.'

The white coated man disappeared around the side of the van as the two sprinted towards it. As they ran round the van they came to a sudden stop. The man in front of them stood smiling, a small snub nosed revolver in his hand.

The man quickly searched Lisa and Jack, confiscating their smartphones. Still smiling he said, 'Any sound, any attempt to attract attention and I'll stop the van and shoot you both. Now get in.'

Jack looked at him, weighing him up. He was taller than Jack, very thin, with a grey pallor about his face that spoke to some kind of skin malaise. Jack felt his heavier weight would be an advantage in a straight fight but the thin man was almost half Jack's age, which would ultimately give the younger man the upper-hand. One quick heavy punch should knock him down but he still had the gun. Getting in the van was the last thing Jack wanted. He looked at Lisa and hoped she had the same thought. The wink from Jack was confirmation. As she moved to enter the van she feigned a stumble and fell, the man took his eyes off Jack and that was all he needed.

Jack's open hand chopped down on the man's gun hand, dislodging the weapon and breaking the wrist. The left fist was already on its way and it caught the man square on the point of his chin, knocking him off his feet. Lisa scrabbled under the van, searching for the gun as Jack kicked his opponent hard in the ribs, knocking the breath from his lungs. The man rolled over into a foetal position, gasping for air. Jack stepped closer and gave him another vicious kick in the kidneys. The fake doctor lay there groaning, as Lisa crawled out from under the van, revolver in hand.

'You okay?'

She grinned. 'I'm good. Impressive, Mr Castle. Not bad at all for an old man.'

'Hrrm . . . 'Less of the, old man.'

The skinny guy was still moaning as Jack unceremoniously retrieved their phones from the pocket of the white coat. He took the gun from Lisa. 'Call the police,' he said as he handed her the phone, then gave the moaning, would be assailant, another kick. 'Get the fuck up.'

The man struggled to his knees, then slowly stood upright. Jack moved back. 'Okay, shithead, this way.'

As they moved from behind the van a single shot rang out. The side of the man's head disintegrated, splattering blood and brain matter over the adjacent wall. Jack instinctively ducked back behind the vehicle, then watched, as the dead man slid down the wall and onto the concrete floor.

The screech of tyres preceded the big 4x4 as it raced for the up-ramp. Jack caught the first couple of numbers of the licence plate but, more importantly saw it was a military vehicle.

At the Bethesda Central Precinct, Lisa and Jack made their statements. Their stories remained the same as they'd told the sergeant at the air-base; they were friends of Captain Bergen and had come to the hospital to see how he was. Jack had suspected the fake doctor and had pursued when they found Bergen dead.

The police were surprised why the Englishman was intuitive enough to chase the murderer and competent enough to disarm him, until he told them he was ex British Army. The interviewing detective was even more surprised when the Police Captain came into the room and said they were to be released immediately they'd finished their statements.

After Jack and Lisa left the precinct, the detective went to see his boss. 'Who the fuck were those two?'

The captain looked at his colleague. 'Not sure, but they have friends in high places, so my guess is spooks. She's probably CIA and the British guy, MI6.'

The captain took a sip from a steaming mug of coffee. 'And I reckon there's a lot more going on here than those two just visiting a sick friend.'

Chapter Twenty Two
'The Bistro'

It was late afternoon by the time they got back to Lisa's apartment. Jack took out his smartphone then looked at his Rolex.

'You calling Nicole?' said Lisa.

'It's after midnight in the Gulf. I'll leave it until morning. Gonna give Mathew a bell though.'

'You want to eat out tonight?' she asked.

'Yeah sure.'

'There's a cool bistro a couple of blocks down, we'll go there. I'm gonna get a shower.'

Jack smiled and nodded, then swiped the screen.

'Jack. How are you doing?'

'Hi, Matt. We're good. We tracked down Captain Bergen.'

'Excellent, well done.'

'Don't get too excited, bro. He's dead.'

Jack reported all the day's events, from the air-base to the police precinct.

Mathew cleared his throat. 'Scuse me. Now there's only one name left on the list.'

'Yes. Have you guys come up with any ideas where we can find him, Matt?'

'Lieutenant Colonel Marcus Nelson spent most of his career in Military Intelligence, Jack.'

'Yeah, I know.'

'If he doesn't want to be found, it's highly likely we won't find him. Nelson is gone. There is no Nelson.'

'Okay, we still have plenty of evidence. It would've been better if we had a live witness but we're still in the game. It's not over yet.'

'Has Lisa spoken to her controller?'

'Not yet. We're gonna see him in the morning. We'd have still been in police custody if he hadn't bailed us out. He's not impressed at the moment, being kept in the dark.'

'What you going to tell him, Jack?'

'Lisa and I will talk about it tonight and decide.'

'Okay, bro, you take care. It's a high stakes game you're playing.'

'Don't I know it. I'll be in touch. Thanks, Mathew.'

'Bye, Jack.'

The line went dead.

He'd showered and changed and was sitting watching the news on TV. President Elect Alex Mason's inauguration was now only a few days away and almost every channel reported the coming event.

Lisa came in. 'You ready?'

She wore a deep blue silk dress with a large floral motif, which showed off her athletic figure perfectly.

'Wow, you look terrific.'

She smiled, feigned a curtsey and in an over affected southern-drawl said, 'Why thank you kind, sir.'

As he held the door open he inhaled her perfume. 'Hmm . . . Christian Dior, nice.'

The bistro was set back from the road with a small garden at the front. The handsome young man at the

103

desk greeted Lisa. 'Good evening, madam. Nice to see you, again.'

'Thank you, Paul, We haven't booked. Can you squeeze us in, please?'

The man smiled, clearly smitten with Lisa. 'Of course, madam. This way please.'

The host picked up some menus and led the way to a nicely situated table towards the rear of the dining area. Once they were seated he handed them the menus. 'We have some very nice sea bass fresh in and Antonio's special this evening is a classic, Tournedos Rossini.'

Lisa flashed the smile. 'Thank you, Paul, sounds lovely.'

'Can I get you something to drink?'

'A large glass of white Chianti, please.'

'Sir?'

'Sparkling water. A large bottle, please.'

Paul smiled and retreated for the drinks.

'Oh, he's definitely got the hots for you, babe.'

Lisa frowned. 'Behave.'

By mid-evening the bistro had filled up. A trio had appeared and were playing smooth jazz tunes, which had several couples swaying rhythmically on the tiny dance floor. They'd eaten the sea bass and the Rossini and while Jack enjoyed the dessert, Lisa sipped at her third Chianti.

'Can you dance, Jack?'

Jack wiped his mouth with the linen napkin. 'Can I dance? When I was a lot younger we used to go to the Twisted Wheel in Manchester. It was a dance club; the place where Northern Soul music originated. We used to work all day and then drive two hours from the Lake District to Manchester, then dance all night. But that was forty-odd years ago.'

She pushed her chair back, stood up and with a hand on her hip. 'So is that a yes or a no?'

'It's a yes.'

They joined the small group on the dance floor and the rhythm took over. 'Not a bad mover for an old man.'

'That's the second time you've called me an old man today, lady.'

She leaned in, kissed his cheek and smiled. 'Oh, I think you're far from anything like old, Mr Castle.'

It was dark when they left the bistro, the temperature had dropped but it was still very pleasant. Lisa linked her arm through his and as they sauntered back, turned to him, 'This could almost have been a date, honey.'

He squeezed her arm in his. 'Another time, another life and it certainly could have been.'

They both laughed . . ., until the man behind them pushed the gun into Jack's back, 'Get in the alley-way.'

Chapter Twenty Three
'Call Me Marcus'

The alley was actually a small service entrance to one of the apartment buildings; dark and narrow, with a row of dumpsters along one side.

'Keep walking,' the voice was quiet, calm.

They passed the dumpsters. 'Okay, stop. Hands against the wall.'

They did as instructed and waited as the man quickly searched them. 'Okay, turn around.'

Even in the gloom, Jack recognised him from the photos in Charlie Webster's dossier. 'Lieutenant Colonel, Marcus Nelson. I thought you'd be taller?'

Jack could see Nelson smile. 'And you're, Jack Castle.'

'Yeah, this is Lisa Reynard.'

'I know who she is. And I know what you guys have been up to. You've been a busy man, Mr Castle.'

'Call me, Jack. If you know what we've been up to, then you'll know why we needed to find you?'

Nelson looked towards the alleyway entrance. 'I know everyone who had anything to do with the Afghan opium deal is dead. All except me and our esteemed president-to-be, that is.'

Jack said, 'Colonel Nelson, we need you to testify to the events in Kabul and Alex Mason's involvement in masterminding the operation.'

Nelson smiled again. 'Call me, Marcus. The minute I surface, I'm a dead man too.'

'Okay, listen. First can you put the gun away?'

Nelson seemed to relax. 'Oh, yeah sure.'

'Let's get you to a secure location, and then we work out how to take this fucker down.'

'I can arrange a safe-house,' said Lisa.

'No thank you. No offence, Lisa, but the NSA may not be as secure as you think.'

Jack took her arm. 'He's right. I have a better idea. But first we need to go get your car, Lisa.'

Marcus shook his head. 'No. You're being followed, Jack.'

Jack looked at Lisa, then the colonel. 'By who?'

Nelson looked towards the alley entrance again. 'Not sure. But I picked you up when you arrived in Dulles yesterday. I've been watching you since you arrived in Washington, Jack. And today there is definitely another party interested in you. I have a car a couple of blocks away, near Rock Creek Park. I'll drive into the park and meet you by the fountain in thirty minutes. Don't be late.'

Jack nodded. 'Okay, we'll see you there.'

Marcus took out the gun again. 'Let me check we're good to go. Then follow me outta here in a minute or two.'

They waited as Nelson checked the street, turned and gave them a thumbs-up, then disappeared around the corner. A couple of minutes later they too emerged from the alleyway. There was no sign of the colonel. Jack looked up and down the street. Several couples, a guy on a bicycle, another jogging and the cars on the road; but no one who looked like a threat or a tail.

'They could be anyone,' said Lisa.

'Yeah. Okay let's get to your place, babe.'

It was almost eleven o'clock and the temperature had dropped considerably. The Park was deserted and the small roads that ran through it were empty. Jack and Lisa sat on the bench across from the fountain, arms around each other, as if they were lovers. They'd only been there for about five minutes when Nelson's car arrived. Lisa quickly climbed in the back as Jack got in the front seat. The car smelled strongly of stale cigarette smoke and there was a large crack across the centre of the windscreen.

Jack frowned and tried to wind down the window. 'Bloody hell, Marcus, how long have you had this heap of junk?'

Nelson winked. 'About twenty minutes. I just stole it. Okay, where to, Jack?'

'The British Embassy.'

The car rattled away from the fountain and Nelson said, 'Will we get in there?'

Jack grinned. 'Probably not in this piece of shit but don't worry, it's all arranged.'

Chapter Twenty Four
'Got Any Bourbon?'

The British Embassy is located on Massachusetts Avenue, in the North West area of Washington D.C. The original Ambassador's residence was built by Sir Edwin Lutyens and faces the street and in front of this imposing building stands a striking statue of Winston Churchill. The central embassy building however, is far newer and decidedly less impressive.

The car pulled up to the main gate, as a British security officer came out of the small discreet gatehouse. 'Good evening. How may I help you?'

Jack leaned across from the passenger's seat. 'Evening. My name's Jack Castle. I'm here with Lisa Reynard and Marcus Nelson. We're expected.'

'May I have your ID's please?'

After collecting the documents, the guard retreated to the gate house. Lisa watched as the man made a phone call. Returning to the car he handed back their documents. 'No need to sign-in, sir. You are indeed expected. Through the gate, please, then to the left of that building. Someone will be there waiting for you. Have a nice evening.'

'Thank you,' said Nelson, as the gate slid open.

The colonel stopped the car under a covered parking area next to the building. A side door opened and a casually dressed man in his thirties emerged. 'Jack Castle?'

Jack offered his hand. 'I'm, Castle.'

The man smiled and shook hands. 'Hello, I'm Andrew Gibson.'

'This is Lisa Reynard and Colonel Marcus Nelson.'

'A pleasure.' Gibson lingered over the handshake with Lisa. 'Let's get you guys inside.'

As the electronic door clicked shut behind them, Gibson turned to Jack. 'Mathew sends his regards.'

Nelson leaned towards Lisa, a quizzical look on his face. 'Mathew?'

Lisa spoke quietly. 'Jack's brother.'

The frown remained on the colonel's face. Lisa continued. 'MI6 in London. Mathew arranged this.'

Nelson smiled slightly. 'Right.'

They followed Gibson upstairs and into a large office, where they were greeted by an older man, again in casual wear. Gibson said, 'This is Ken Lonsdale, our Station Chief.'

The man behind the desk stood up. Gibson made the introductions. 'This is, Jack Castle, Lisa Reynard and Colonel Nelson.'

They all shook hands. 'Pleasure to meet you, Jack. Your brother Mathew and I are old friends. He sends his regards, by the way.'

Jack smiled. 'Thank you, sir. Andrew has already passed on Mathew's message.'

'Please, call me Ken.' He indicated a pair of couches facing each other. 'Let's all have a seat. Anyone like anything to drink?'

'You got any Bourbon?' said Nelson.

Lonsdale smiled. 'We have indeed. Andrew would you mind?'

110

Gibson opened a section of wall to reveal a small bar, found the right bottle and poured a substantial amount of the amber liquid into a crystal glass. Handing it to Nelson he said, 'Anyone else?'

There were no takers.

The Section Chief leaned back into the big leather Chesterfield. 'Right, Jack, what can we do for you?'

Chapter Twenty Five
'The Controller'

It was almost two in the morning when the car pulled into the basement parking of Lisa's apartment building. Andrew Gibson had insisted on driving them back to Lisa's place. The Embassy man was clearly smitten with her and after saying, 'Good night.' Suggested they, 'Meet up for lunch some time?'

Lisa's response was a noncommittal smile.

As the Embassy man drove away Jack turned to her. 'Another conquest there, Miss Reynard.'

With a wink, she said, 'Too young for me, hun.'

They rode the elevator to her floor in silence and once in the flat she turned to him. 'You want some tea or anything before bed?'

He looked at his Rolex. 'Not this time of night, babe. I'm gonna get a quick shower then sleep. It's been an eventful day.'

'It certainly has. What's the plan for tomorrow?'

'Now that Nelson is safely tucked up in the Embassy, we'll go see your controller in the morning. Tell him the full story. See what he thinks our next move should be. That's pretty much it.'

She nodded. 'Okay. And the next day your Mafia chum arrives.'

Jack raised his eye brows. 'That's gonna be fun.'

She leaned in and kissed his cheek. 'Okay. Goodnight.'

'Night, Lisa. Thanks for all you're doing.'

'Wouldn't miss it for the world.' Before she left the room she turned. 'Just one thing that's worrying me. Nelson said he thinks we're being followed. I haven't noticed anything but then again I haven't been looking. And you don't seem to be too concerned?'

Jack shrugged his shoulders. 'Nelson could be wrong. And until we know for sure, we stay vigilant. Nothing else we can do. Don't worry. Get some sleep.'

'Yeah, I guess so. Night, Jack.'

The next morning there was a light rain, so breakfast was eaten in the dining room. Jack had, as usual, only slept for a few hours and was up before six o'clock. He'd made a long call to Nicole and giggled on the phone with his daughters.

His second call to Mathew was nowhere near as lighthearted. He'd told him Colonel Nelson was now secure in the Embassy and how he'd made a statement, on video, attesting to Alexander Mason's involvement in masterminding the Afghan opium conspiracy.

Thanks to Alexie Kuragin, they now had the Cayman bank accounts into which the money from the Russians was paid and, although the murders of those involved could not be laid directly at Mason's door it was fair to say everyone, with the exception of Nelson, had been killed at the behest of the President Elect. What Jack did not tell his brother was Vanya Kuragin was on his way to Washington and what that might mean.

Again, at the insistence of Jack, they took Lisa's Porsche for the drive out to Fort Meade. By late morning the rain had become quite heavy, although the temperature remained pleasant.

Although Fort Meade is primarily an American Military Base, it does house several other security agencies, the most important being the National Security Agency or, as it's widely known, the NSA.

Lisa Reynard had been recruited by the agency after the twin towers had come down on 9/11. Prior to that she'd undertaken a few very minor jobs, mostly intelligence gathering and surveillance work, when she was on assignment for the Washington Post in Africa. After being trained in field craft, weapons and tactics, she was now being used more and more. Her position as a respected journalist provided an excellent 'front' and provided the perfect cover while undertaking covert missions for the NSA around the world.

At eleven o'clock precisely they were shown into the offices of Lisa's controller, Gerry McKinnon.

'Lisa, good morning. And this is, Mr Jack Castle?'

As they shook hands Jack said, 'Pleasure to meet you, sir. Please call me Jack. And thank you for expediting our release from the police yesterday.'

McKinnon nodded towards a round table and chairs in the corner. 'Let's have a seat. You want anything to drink before we start?'

Lisa shook her head. 'Nothing for me, sir.'

Jack raised a hand. 'I'm fine, thank you.'

'Okay, Jack, I take it yesterday's little episode has a lot to do with your reason for being here in Washington?'

'It does, sir.'

'Then why don't you start at the beginning?'

Almost two hours later Gerry McKinnon leaned back in his chair. 'Wow. That's some story, Jack.'

'I know it's hard to believe, sir. But the evidence is definitely pointing to it all being true.'

'But the elimination of anyone involved greatly reduces the possibility of corroboration.'

'We still have Colonel Nelson, sir.'

'Yes indeed, but only one man.'

Lisa looked at her boss. 'Nevertheless, sir, the documentation, the bank accounts, the murders of everyone on the list. We even have the Russians confirming they bought and took delivery of the opium. It's all extremely compelling.'

McKinnon stood up and walked around the office. 'We need to get this all to the FBI and Colonel Nelson should be taken into protective custody.'

Jack frowned. 'With respect, sir, we have no idea who is still involved. Yes, all the original conspirators have been eliminated, with the exception of Nelson but there is obviously powerful people still working with Alexander Mason. People who are working to eradicate any connection Mason had with the whole affair.'

Lisa stood up. 'We could be losing the last living witness if we hand the colonel over to the Fed's, sir. Can't we keep him secure here at Fort Meade?'

The controller shook his head. 'This is not in our jurisdiction, Lisa.'

'What about going to the Attorney General?' said Jack.

'No. We have to give this to the Bureau.'

The controller went to his desk and sat down. He tapped the intercom and a metallic voice said, 'Yes, sir?'

'Martha, please put me through to the Director of the FBI.'

Chapter Twenty Six
'The Library'

In Georgia, the Mason family's ancestral home had been renamed, indeed re-branded and was now referred to as an estate, not a plantation. Once named *Pride of Georgia* and subsequent to the abolition of slavery, the shrewd Mason family elected to move with the times. In 1867 the old plantation name was taken down from over the main entrance and replaced with something more politically correct. The sign now read, *The Magnolia Estate*.

The original cotton plantation was now landscaped with cultivated gardens, fountains and orchards. The old buildings, where once a dozen thoroughbreds were stabled, had been converted to a large garage facility, housing a small fleet of high-end vehicles and the living quarters, where over a hundred slaves once existed, had been replaced by a small helicopter landing pad, control room and maintenance workshop. At the side of the helipad stood a brand new Jet-Ranger helicopter.

The huge white house itself was to say the least imposing, with its gleaming columns and the drive up to it, flanked by over a dozen Magnolia trees resembled *Tara*, in *Gone With The Wind*. The Mason family had owned the original plantation since before the American Civil War and after the abolition of slavery, the house and estate had reverted to no more than an opulent home within beautiful grounds.

Every male member of the Mason dynasty had entered and become successful in the military. In 1865, his great, great grandfather was killed at the Battle of Gettysburg. His grandfather fought in Europe during Wold War One and his father was in the first wave to land on Omaha Beach on D-Day.

General Alexander Stonewall Mason was the latest in this great bloodline. His career after university had begun at West Point Military Academy and after entering the Marine Corp as a Lieutenant, rose quickly through the ranks, thanks to hard work, determination and the Mason family name. His reputation as an outstanding but occasionally reckless officer grew in Viet Nam. In Operation Desert Storm he commanded his men alongside General Norman Schwarzkopf and Mason was one of the first Americans into Baghdad following the defeat of Saddam Hussein. His illustrious career continued and ended in Afghanistan, after which, with the support of his wife's influential family, he'd turned to politics. Mason had made many powerful friends during his short diplomatic career and as a US Senator had become a formidable politician and diplomat. The last year however had been spent canvassing successfully for the Presidency.

The sun was setting over the tree covered hills to the west of the estate. The big patio doors were open and the perfume from the evening jasmine filled the room with its distinctive aroma. The library resembled an English gentlemen's club, resplendent with polished wood panelling and shelves stacked from floor to ceiling, holding thousands of fine leather bound tomes. A marble fire place, reputedly brought from Europe, dominated the room and above it hung a life-size portrait of Mason's great, great grandfather, Augustus. Two huge leather sofas faced each in front of the fireplace and several high-backed wing chairs were spread around the elegant space. Fresh flowers on small antique tables softened the overtly masculine domain, their scent overpowered by the heady fragrance from the jasmine.

In his early sixties, Alexander Mason was an imposing figure. Tall, slim, with a full head of silver hair and eyes that sparkled, yet showed little emotion. He was well educated and smart but lacked any sense of humour. As an officer he'd been respected, almost revered, by the men who'd served with him and his bravery and leadership were legend, all of which added to his charismatic presence.

Mason, dressed in an evening suit, stood with one hand on the high mantle of the fireplace, in the other he held a large Monte Cristo. As he puffed at the cigar, the grey-blue smoke floated upwards and dissipated above his head. The other man also wore an evening suit and was seated on the big sofa, sipping from a crystal brandy balloon. As he swirled the amber liquid he sniffed at the rim of the glass. Mason moved from the fireplace and sat opposite his guest. 'You've done well up to now. But yesterday's fiasco was unacceptable.'

The man took a gulp of the fine Cognac and looked sheepishly over the rim. 'I agree, General. The situation did get slightly out of control but the target was eliminated and the backup ensured our man was not captured, sir.'

Mason took another deep draw on the cigar and watched the smoke drift upwards. 'Yes, yes. About this intervention, as you put it. These two people, this man and woman. They seem to have a great interest in our business and a lot more knowledge than we would like. What can you tell me about them?'

'Not much at the moment but I've made arrangements to have them removed from the equation, General.'

'I'm not sure that would be wise until we know all about them. I think you need to find out all they know before they are, as you say, removed from the equation.'

'Of course, sir. My plan is to resolve this interruption quickly and then focus our energies on finding Colonel Nelson.'

The heavy door opened, ending their conversation. The two men stood, as Elizabeth Rhodes-Mason approached them. 'Gentlemen, enough talking. It's time for dinner.'

Mason laid the cigar in a big crystal ashtray and smiled at his wife. 'Elizabeth, yes of course. Sorry, my dear. We're coming now.' Then turning to the other man. 'Let me know how things go.'

The man smiled. 'Yes, of course, General.'

The woman stopped abruptly, a stern look on her face. 'General?' then her look softened and a broad smile appeared. 'Mr President, if you don't mind.'

They all laughed.

Chapter Twenty Seven
'Here They Come'

In Washington, the rain had persisted all night but the morning brought clear skies and bright sunshine. The meeting with Lisa's controller had gone reasonably well. Jack had agreed to hand over all documentation and evidence from his smartphone and promised to ensure the originals would be couriered from London. The FBI Deputy Director, a particularly arrogant and self-important individual, would personally oversee the transfer of Colonel Nelson from the British Embassy to a Bureau safe-house.

Nelson was due to be transferred at eight o'clock that morning. Jack had asked to be allowed to travel with Nelson on the journey to the safe house but the Deputy Director was adamant they, the FBI, were now in charge. Although Jack had done a sterling job in amassing the evidence, his services were no longer required. This was an American issue and Jack should have no more involvement.

Vanya Kuragin had messaged Jack confirming he'd arrived in Washington and would be at the Lincoln Memorial at noon as planned. It was a little after six-thirty when Jack and Lisa finished breakfast and as he cleared the table he said, 'We have plenty of time before I meet Kuragin. Let's go to the Embassy. At least we can see Nelson off.'

'I'm not sure, honey. That FBI joker made it clear they didn't need any more from us.'

'Fuck him. We brought Nelson in. The least we can do is see him off.'

She knew it was pointless to argue. 'Okay.'

By seven thirty Jack and Lisa were seated with Colonel Nelson in the Section Chief's office at the British Embassy. Jack could see Nelson was nervous as he sipped at his mug of coffee. Ken Lonsdale, in immaculate three piece business suit stood at the window. He too appeared far less relaxed than the previous night. The chit-chat in the room was of no importance as the four awaited the arrival of the FBI transfer team. Just before eight o'clock Lonsdale turned from the window and said, 'Here they come.'

Six large black 4x4's pulled up to the secure side of the Embassy building. Lonsdale returned to his desk and sat down. A few minutes later his assistant, Andrew Gibson entered with the Deputy Director of the FBI and three other men. Jack looked at the three agents and repressed a smile. They were all dressed in business suits and sunglasses. He leaned close to Lisa and whispered 'Looks like a bloody jazz trio.'

Handshakes were exchanged between the Section Chief and the Deputy but Jack and Lisa were only afforded a cursory nod from the arrogant man.

The FBI boss stood in the centre of the room and said, 'Okay, this is how it's gonna work. We have six vehicles. These will be split into three separate convoys. You, Colonel Nelson, will travel in one of them. Once the vehicles exit the Embassy grounds they will disperse and your convoy will get you to our most secure safe house. Okay? Any questions?'

Marcus Nelson stood up and shook hands with Jack and Lisa. 'Thanks. I hope to see you again.'

Jack nodded. 'Yeah. me too. Take care, Marcus.'

The Deputy Director clapped his hands. 'Okay, let's get this show on the road.'

In the secure parking area Jack and Lisa watched as the colonel climbed into the last of the six vehicles. Nelson flicked a salute just as the door was pulled shut. Through the blacked-out window he saw Jack's hand raised in acknowledgment.

Before he left the Embassy, Jack called his brother Mathew and, although still the middle of the night in England, the phone was answered immediately.

'Jack. Hi there.'

'Morning, Mathew. Hope I didn't wake you?'

'No. I was waiting for your call. How did it go?'

'Yeah, went okay I guess. The Feds have just picked up the Colonel. We decided to see him off from the Embassy.'

Mathew cleared his throat. 'Okay good. Well, that's it I suppose? It's in the hands of the Americans now. When are you coming back?'

'I'll hang on a day or two and let you know,' said Jack.

'Okay, stay in touch. And stay out of trouble. It's not our problem now.'

'Yeah, right. Okay, bye for now, Matt.'

Instead of going back to Lisa's apartment they drove into the city. The day was warming up after the previous night's rain and the heat from the sun in the clear blue sky was tempered by a light breeze, making for a very pleasant morning. The roads were busy as usual but as they weren't in any particular hurry Jack sat back, happy to be driven around the monuments like a tourist. Eventually they ended up in Georgetown. They parked up and walked down to the Potomac River, found a table in an open-air café in front of the Watergate Hotel and ordered a Cappuccino and a Coke.

'You want me to come with you to meet Kuragin?' said Lisa.

Jack shook his head. 'No, I don't think so. He's unpredictable enough as it is. I'll talk to him alone. But you should definitely be close by.'

She smiled and then winked. 'Okay, honey. I'll watch your back.'

Jack laughed just as Lisa's smartphone beeped.

'Hello. Lisa Reynard.'

Jack watched as her smile slowly faded. 'Yes, sir. Yes, sir. Of course, sir. Yes, we'll be there later today. Yes of course. Thank you, sir. Goodbye.'

'What is it?' said Jack.

Lisa looked at the phone for several seconds then turned to him, eyes narrowed. 'The FBI convoy was hit when it arrived at the safe house. Nelson's dead.'

Chapter Twenty Eight
'75 Minutes Earlier'

As they left the Embassy grounds Marcus Nelson watched as the convoy of six vehicles swiftly divided into three. Two vehicles headed north, two more towards the city and Nelson's cars took the main road to the east. There were no sirens or flashing lights but the small convoy moved quickly through the streets and headed out towards Virginia. In the lead vehicle were three agents and a driver. Nelson, the Deputy Director and a couple more FBI men travelled behind.

It didn't take long to get out of the city and onto Highway 66 towards the small town of Oakton. The FBI boss had very little to say on the journey and although polite, his demeanour was not particularly friendly. There were no comments from the other occupants of the vehicle and the trip passed in relative silence.

Marcus watched as the Virginia countryside flashed by either side of the six lane highway, his thoughts of what may happen over the coming days foremost in his mind. He closed his eyes for a few seconds, took a deep breath and composed himself, resigned to the momentous events yet to come. The vehicle changing direction and leaving the highway made him open his eyes, just in time to see the sign for OAKTON flash past.

Oakton, with its population of around thirty thousand, is an affluent suburb of Washington, about twenty miles east of the city. The beautifully appointed town, with its tree lined streets and attractive houses, is located conveniently for commuters just off Route 66 in central Fairfax County.

On entering the town proper, the small convoy slowed to normal speed as it passed though the busy little borough. Out to the north of town they joined a smaller road which followed the river towards Lake Amelia.

'Nice location,' said Nelson.

The Deputy, turned to him. 'Sure is. Really nice. But I prefer the city. Only time I wanna be out here is to do some huntin.'

The colonel nodded to the man. 'Right.' Then turned and looked out the window, under his breath he said, 'Asshole.'

The lead driver's voice came over the radio. 'Two minutes to location, sir.'

The FBI chief smiled for the first time that morning. 'Soon have you secured now, Colonel. All nice and easy.'

Nelson continued to look out through the blacked-out glass. 'Seems like it.'

The two vehicles turned off the road and onto a small driveway, giving Nelson his first glimpse of the safe-house. The old wooden building looked quaint sitting right on the lake's edge, its covered porch jutting out over the water. The surrounding gardens were a little over grown but the building itself look substantial and well maintained.

Fifty yards offshore, a small motor launch moved slowly on the shimmering water, its wake spreading gently behind it. The vehicles came to a stop alongside the building, just as the driver shouted, 'Incoming. Incoming.'

The rocket streaked from the small launch, its golden flame reflected on the smooth service of the lake. The speeding projectile found its target and the lead vehicle disappeared in a thunderous explosion. The shock wave reverberated through Nelson's vehicle as the Deputy Director screamed, 'Disperse. Disperse.'

The driver rammed the car into reverse and through a cloud of swirling dust and spinning wheels tried to back away from the killing zone.

'Oh, god,' yelled the FBI boss, as the second rocket streaked towards them.

Chapter Twenty Nine
'The Lincoln Memorial'

At the riverside café, Jack and Lisa sat in silence. Then she said, 'This is crazy.'

Jack leaned back in his chair and looked up to the sky. 'Jesus, Lisa. What the hell happened?'

'My controller wants us to go up to Fort Meade later today. He'll give us a full briefing.'

'What did he say just now?'

Lisa looked around and then leaned forward, her arms on the table. 'Nelson's convoy was hit as soon as it arrived at the safe house. There were two agents in the house and they saw the whole thing. A small boat was on the lake. It took out both vehicles with a couple of rockets.'

'Any survivors?'

'No, Jack. They killed Marcus Nelson and the Deputy Director, as well as six agents.'

Jack shook his head slightly. 'There's no stopping this bastard.'

'I'm really worried now,' said Lisa. 'We're the only two people alive that know the whole story.'

'No we're not. The Russians know and when I meet Vanya they'll know a lot more.'

Lisa looked at her watch. 'We'd better go and meet him then.'

The Lincoln Memorial is one of the most famous buildings in the world. Situated at the western end of the

National Mall and surrounded by parkland, it took eight years to build and was opened to the public in 1922. Since then, millions of Americans and foreign tourist have visited the iconic building.

After parking the car Jack and Lisa entered Memorial Park separately. She headed to the tree covered area away from the front of the building and Jack walked towards the marble steps leading up to the memorial itself. He looked at his Rolex, eleven-fifty-five.

Lisa found a seat on one of the many benches available and took out her smartphone. She feigned flicking through the screen as she kept her eye on Jack. She looked around and felt sure she saw someone she recognised but then the figure was gone into a crowd of tourists. She stood up and looked in every direction; scrutinising the faces of the dozens of people milling around the popular tourist site. *Maybe we're being followed?* She sat down and looked for Jack, then saw him at the foot of the gleaming white steps, Vanya Kuragin at his side.

Jack held out his hand. 'Vanya. Thank you for coming.'

The offered handshake was not accepted. The Russian looked nervous. 'I'm here. Now tell me who killed my father?'

Jack nodded. 'Let's take a walk.'

As they moved away from the monument, Lisa saw two other men follow at a distance. She smiled, *Kuragin's minders,* then stood and held the smartphone to her ear, continuing the pretence of chatting; she too followed at a distance. She watched Jack and the Russian for several minutes, Jack doing almost all the talking.

Suddenly Vanya stopped and turned to Jack, the look on the young mafia boss's face spoke volumes.

Again the two men began walking, Kuragin's minders and Lisa following at a distance. A large group of Japanese tourists passed between her and Jack and again she was sure she recognised a face in the group. The man wore a baseball cap and sunglasses but there was something about him. She looked again but, as before, the stranger was gone.

Jack and Vanya had talked for almost twenty minutes and were now back at the foot of the memorial's steps. Lisa watched the couple as heads were nodded and then, to her surprise, a handshake. She waited as Kuragin walked away; his two minders swiftly joined him. Jack also watched until the small Russian group were out of sight.

As Jack approached, Lisa resumed her seat on the bench. As he sat down she said, 'That all looked very buddy-buddy?'

He grinned slightly. 'Yeah, went well. Better than I'd hoped actually.'

'So what's our next move, Mr Castle?'

He smiled. 'I'm going to New York, babe.'

Lisa turned and frowned. 'And what's in New York?'

Jack looked into her eyes. 'I'm gonna meet Mr Sasha Kuragin. Vanya's uncle.'

Lisa linked her arm with his as they strolled back to the carpark. A hundred yards away the man in the baseball cap stepped out from behind a large oak tree, a smartphone to his ear. 'They're heading back to the car.'

As Lisa drove out of the busy parking area she said, 'So when are we going to New York?'

Jack had his smartphone out. He held up his hand. 'Hold on, I'm gonna call Mathew. Let him know about Colonel Nelson's death.'

'Okay.'

The phone beeped for several seconds and then. 'Jack. Hello. How're you doing? '

'Hi, Mathew. I'm fine, but not good news I'm afraid. The Colonel was killed earlier today.'

The line went silent.

'Mathew?'

'Yeah, I'm here, Jack. This is bad. Means there are elements in the FBI involved with the cover-up as well as the military.'

'Looks like it,' said Jack. 'The only people who knew which safe-house was gonna be used were the Feds.'

Mathew coughed. 'Scuse me. That's right. I think you need to get the hell back here now, Jack. You're risking far too much.'

'You could be right, bro. But the inauguration is only a few days away. I'm gonna hang on until then.'

'That's not smart, Jack.'

Jack laughed. 'If I were smart I'd be in the fancy office in London and you'd be here.'

'Okay, listen. If you're hell bent on staying, then just keep your head down. There's not really anything more you can do.'

Jack looked up as they drove past the Washington Monument. The huge obelisk gleamed in the afternoon sun. 'Maybe your right, bro. Okay I gotta go. Talk soon, Matt.'

'You be safe, Jack.'

The line went dead.

Lisa weaved in and out of the busy traffic. 'Mathew telling you to get the hell out?'

Jack looked at her. 'Yep. Thinks there's no more we can do.'

'And you've still not told him about the Russians?'

'No. Better he doesn't know. For now anyway.'

She beeped the horn at a Kamikaze cyclist as he shot between her and a taxi. 'Speaking of Russians you've still not told me why we're going to New York.'

'Not we, babe,' said Jack. 'You gotta go see your boss at Fort Meade. 'I'll go to meet Vanya and his uncle alone.'

'Is that wise?'

Jack grinned. 'Who the hell knows? But Vanya wants me to go and tell the whole story to his uncle.'

She shook her head slightly. 'I don't like it, Jack.'

'Don't worry. I know what I'm doing. I think.'

'When are you going?'

'Now. You can drop me off at Union Station. I'll get the next train up there. I'll meet with the old uncle and be back here as soon as I can.'

'Okay, honey. Union Station it is.'

Chapter Thirty
'The Entrepreneur'

Lisa pulled up right in front of Union Station. Jack quickly climbed out before the traffic cop had a chance to move her on.

'I'll call you after the meeting and let you know what train I'll be back on.'

She nodded as the traffic cop approached. 'Okay. Be careful eh?'

Jack grinned as the Porsche's tyres squealed away from the sidewalk. The apologetic wave from Lisa brought a smile to the cop's face as she sped off.

Union Station is the main railway hub for Washington and the East Coast. The high-speed trains that run between DC and New York usually make the journey in less than three hours, unfortunately as Jack had to queue for a ticket, he missed the express. The next train north would be a regular service leaving in forty five minutes and would get him to Penn Station a little after five-thirty in the afternoon.

The First Class carriages were busy but Jack still managed to get a seat in the dining car section, where he was pleasantly surprised to find the tables set with linen cloths, fine china and high quality flatware. The menu, although small, was perfectly acceptable and on reading through it he found himself wanting and ready to enjoy a relaxed meal.

He was seated opposite a bespectacled young man in his twenties who, during the course of the journey, explained he was the designer of a new smartphone application which allowed couples to meet on-line. Jack was mildly impressed when his travelling companion said he was on his way to New York to sell his application to Google.

Jack and the young entrepreneur enjoyed a very respectable lunch, after which and without going into any specifics Jack mentioned the problem he was having finding a solution to the Afghan conspiracy. The young man listened and after Jack had encapsulated the story, again without specifics his travelling companion said, 'You've heard of Occam's Razor, haven't you, Jack?'

Jack smiled. 'I've heard the term but I have to admit I don't really get it.'

The young man cleared his throat and sat up in his seat, as if preparing to give a lecture. 'Occam's Razor basically says, when all other explanations have proved untrue, then the simplest or most obvious explanation is the answer. Be prepared to accept the obvious as being the solution.'

Jack nodded and smiled again. 'Yeah, I guess that's right, don't overlook the obvious. Cheers, son.'

On arrival at Penn Station, Jack left the coach with the young entrepreneur and together they walked to the main exit. As they came through the barrier they saw a liveried chauffeur holding a placard, the name in bold multi-coloured script.

Pointing to the sign the young man said, 'This is me, Jack. Can I give you a lift anywhere?'

134

Jack shook his head slightly. 'No, I'm fine. But thanks anyway. I'll get a cab.'

'Okay. Well it was nice to meet you, sir. Goodbye'

'You too, son. Good luck.'

As Jack waited in the queue, a gleaming stretch limo, its rear window down, slowly passed the taxi rank. Jack smiled and then nodded in response to the young man's wave.

The meeting with the Russians was set for eight o'clock that evening. Jack had taken a cab from Penn Station to the Hilton in central Manhattan. He found a comfortable seat in a corner of one of the lounges and ordered tea. He called Nicole and then checked emails and messages on his smartphone. By seven-thirty he was in another yellow cab and on his way to the address on 5th Avenue.

It was fifteen minutes to eight when the taxi pulled up in front of an elegant multi-storey building overlooking Central Park. Jack paid the cab and walked up the short flight of steps to the huge ornate doors, where he was greeted by a smartly dressed doorman.

'Good evening, sir. May I help you?'

Jack smiled. 'I have a meeting with Mr Kuragin.'

'May I have your name please, sir?'

'Castle, Jack Castle.'

'Thank you, sir. This way please.' The door was opened and Jack entered an impressive, classically decorated hallway. It's floors and columns resplendent in white and grey marble shimmered in the light of a huge glittering chandelier.

There were three elevators. The doorman stopped in front of the third and tapped in a six digit code. As the doors slid silently open, he said, 'This will take you directly to the penthouse, sir.'

Jack stepped into the lift and said, 'Thank you,' as the man leaned in and pushed a button.
A few seconds later the mirrored doors opened and Jack was greeted by a stern faced Vanya Kuragin.

Chapter Thirty One
'Uncle Sasha'

Kuragin's penthouse was actually a duplex apartment that consisted of the entire top two floors of the old building. Jack was surprised to see the place decorated in an ultra-contemporary style with clean lines and stylish Italian furniture, *Classy place*, he thought as Vanya took him into the huge drawing room. The original patio widows were still in place and opened out onto a large balcony, which overlooked the full expanse of Central Park. On the balcony an old man stood, speaking quietly on a cellphone, his back to the room. Vanya waited for the man to finish, then as the man turned and entered the room said, 'This is Jack Castle, uncle. This is my uncle, Sasha Ivanovich Kuragin.'

For a second Jack was stunned, he realised he was staring and offered his hand. 'Pleasure to meet you, sir.'

Kuragin smiled and as they shook hands said, 'You look surprised, Mr Castle?'

Jack nodded slightly. 'Yes, sorry. Excuse me, sir.'

The man standing in front of him was the spitting image of the dead Alexie Kuragin.

'Twins, Mr Castle. Identical twins. Although technically I am older than my brother by seventeen minutes. And please, call me Sasha. May I call you, Jack?'

'Of course, sir. Sasha.'

The old mafia boss smiled. 'Let's have a seat. Can we get you anything to drink, Jack? Vodka? Scotch?'

'No thank you, nothing. I gave up alcohol many years ago.'

'Ah, a man of willpower.'

Jack smiled. 'Not that much.'

'I have to disagree, Jack. I believe you are a man of many virtues.'

'Not so sure that's completely accurate either,' said Jack, smiling.

'Loyalty and courage are the virtues I prize most, my friend. And certainly you have these.'

Jack smiled again. 'Maybe I will have a drink. Water or Coke, please.'

The old man waved his hand. 'Vanya, would you mind? And I'll have a small vodka, please.'

The drinks arrived and Jack raised his glass. 'Nostrovia.'

Kuragin nodded. 'Ah, yes, of course, you speak Russian. You have a beautiful Russian wife and of course your father in-law, the famous Dimitri Mikhailovich Orlov.'

'Your brother had a problem with Dimitri. Does that problem become yours, Sasha?'

The old man laughed. 'Ah, yes, that problem. No, Jack, in this instance the issue between them does not concern me. It was something many years ago when they were young. It was purely a personal matter. Nothing at all to do with business.'

'May I ask what the issue was?'

The Russian smiled. 'There was a fight over a woman in St Petersburg. Long before Dimitri met and married his English wife. But that's all I will say on the matter.

You will have to ask him if you want to know the full story.'

Jack nodded and smiled as well. 'I just might.'

'And talking of the full story, shall we begin, Jack?'

The old man leaned back into the soft leather of the couch. The smiling face turned serious. 'Tell me all you know about the death of my brother and the involvement of our esteemed President Elect?'

The meeting with Sasha Kuragin ended a little after nine-thirty. The old boss had insisted a couple of his men should drive him to Penn Station, a courtesy Jack felt rather uneasy with at first; his imagination ran wild with thoughts of being driven out to some remote location and being left with a bullet in the back of his head. His irrational thoughts proved to be exactly that, when the two mafia men managed to get him to the station in time to catch the ten-fifteen express back to Washington.

Chapter Thirty Two
'Now, Now, Senator'

The hotel suite overlooked Times Square. It was almost two in the morning and the party had been going since midnight. The big bedroom was in a mess, empty Champagne bottles were strewn around the room and an overflowing ashtray had been knocked onto the elegant carpet. The glass coffee table had a light film of dust surrounding several neatly formed lines of white powder. On the huge bed two naked young women writhed and moaned as their bodies intertwined. In the armchair and equally naked, a much older man watched wide eyed, as the sweat covered females wrapped their bodies around each other.

He leaned forward and hunched over the glass table, then with a small golden tube inhaled a line of cocaine into each nostril.

'Ahhhh,' he yelled, as his head went back, eyes closed tight.

The couple on the bed continued their erotic contortions as the man stood, picked up a full bottle of Dom Perignon and then laughing wildly, poured the contents all over the squealing women.

The squeals of surprise turned to shrieks of fear as the door to the room was thrown open and three burly young men entered. The old man turned and in a fit of cocaine induced bravery charged the intruders, the bottle now a weapon in his raised hand.

The unfit and grossly overweight man rushed forward. 'Bastaaards,' he yelled.

The first intruder stepped aside and deftly tripped the lumbering drunk, causing him to crash into the wall. The old man slid to the floor, winded, mouth open. The second young man put a foot on the white flabby chest, pinning the man to the floor. The third man smiled, knelt down and took the bottle from the gasping man's hand. He raised the bottle to his mouth and slurped the few remaining drops of the sparkling liquid, then smiling, said, 'Now, now, Senator. Just stay calm. Mister Kuragin would like a word with you.'

In the penthouse on 5th Avenue, Sasha Kuragin watched as Senator David Ashton drank his third mug of black coffee.

'I think I'm going to be sick,' said the pale faced politician.

The old mafia boss waved his hand. 'Sergei, take this fool to the bathroom.'

Several minutes later the semi sobered man returned, eyes bloodshot red and breathing hard.

Kuragin spoke quietly. 'How are you feeling now, Senator?'

'I feel awful. And why am I here in the middle of the night?'

'Sit down, please,' said Kuragin, quietly.

The shaking man took a seat on the fine leather couch.

'How long have we known each other, David?'

'Can I have some water, please?'

'Sergei, a glass of water, please. So how long, David?'

'I don't know, maybe twelve, thirteen years.' He gulped the water down, coughing as the cool liquid caught in his throat.

'Fifteen years,' said Kuragin. 'We have known each other fifteen years. And in all that time have I not looked after your interests? Especially with your political ambitions.'

'Yes, yes. You have. But I have helped you too, Sasha.'

'Indeed you have and we have both enjoyed the benefits of our mutual support, have we not?'

'Sasha, it's late. I don't feel well. Can't we do this another time?'

The old Russian stood, his voice hard, angry. 'You will do what I want, whenever I want it. Do you understand?'

The bloodshot eyes widened and filled with tears. 'Sasha, please, you should not talk to me like that. I am an American Senator.'

Kuragin stepped forward and leaned menacingly over the trembling man. 'You are a degenerate cocaine addict and a sexual deviant. And you remain a senator because I choose to let you. Do you understand?'

'Yes. Yes, I'm sorry, Sasha.'

The mafia boss resumed his seat, the calm voice returned. 'Sergei, the gift, please.'

A large royal-blue velvet bag, with a golden draw-string was placed on the table between the two men. The senator leaned forward, a puzzled look on his pale face. 'A gift for me?'

Kuragin smiled. 'No, not this time. This is for our new president. You will take it with you when you return to Washington tomorrow.'

The senator tried to speak but the Russian raised his hand. 'You will not open the bag. You will hand the gift to the president in person tomorrow. You will not give it to anyone else. Do you understand?'

The shaking man stood up. Worry and fear were written all over his face. 'Sasha this is not a device is it?'

Kuragin stood and picked up the bag. 'Senator, do you really think we would blow up the new president. Don't be foolish. This is a gift and it is a surprise. You will take it to him and say it is from you.'

'But what's in the bag, Sasha?'

The Russian smiled. 'As I said, David. A surprise. But when he opens it he will be delighted and I assure you, very happy with you for presenting it to him.'

'Very well. But I must get some sleep now. May I go, please?'

'Of course, David, of course. And thank you for stopping by at such a late hour. I will see you very soon in Washington. Sergei, please take the senator back to his hotel.'

With the blue bag under his arm, the senator walked to the door, turned and said, 'Good night, Sasha.'

As the door closed the old Russian said, 'Idiot.'

* * *

Lisa collected Jack from Union Station a little after one o'clock. He'd thought of his young travelling companion earlier in the day and his Occam's Razor theory. He'd then spent the three hour trip going over all the documents stored on his smartphone and was surprised to find something that previously had not been obvious.

On returning to the flat they'd spent almost two hours talking about the meeting with the Russians and the plan Jack had formulated on the journey back to DC. Lisa was to play a key role in that plan and especially in the next day's events.

Chapter Thirty Three
'Emily Harding-West'

Lisa had set breakfast on the balcony and while they ate, she told him how the meeting with her NSA controller had gone and how pissed-off her boss had been when Jack failed to show up. She'd covered his absence by saying he'd succumbed to a nasty bout of food-poisoning and with such unpleasant side effects, was reluctant to leave her apartment.

The President's Inauguration was now only a few days away and all across the Capitol various celebrations were taking place. Not least of these was the victory lunch being held that day by *The Daughters of the Mayflower*.

This auspicious and ancient fraternity had been founded in 1621, one year after The Mayflower landed in the New World. The descendants, or rather the female descendants of the original 130 pilgrims and crew have kept this noble institution alive. Although only a handful of the current membership can actually trace their lineage back to the landing at Plymouth Rock; with the right background and social status, a lady may, with the agreement of all members, become a *Daughter*.

Lisa of course could never belong to this socially elitist circle, certainly not with her Italian heritage but she did have a very good friend who was a member.

Before her marriage to Congressman James West, Emily Harding had attended Princeton University where she and Lisa had become lifelong friends. It was Emily

Harding-West who had agreed to take Lisa to today's celebratory lunch.

Jack had already called Nicole and the girls earlier and was just finishing the call to Mathew, when a few minutes before noon Lisa entered the drawing room.

He stood up. 'Wow. You look terrific, Very classy, ma'am.'

Again she feigned the southern accent and with an overt curtsy said, 'Why thank ya kindly, sir.'

Jack drove Lisa to the Potomac Hilton and planned to find some lounge or bar, in which to while away the time until the lunch was over.

The driveway up to the Hilton main entrance was backed-up with over a dozen limousines and cars as liveried chauffeurs dropped off their passengers. Jack watched as elegant women of all ages disembarked, chatted and made their way into the grand hotel foyer.

'I'll get out here, honey,' said Lisa.

'You sure?'

'Yeah, it's fine. Looks like this will take a while to clear. You go park-up and I'll call you when I'm ready to leave.'

Jack grinned. 'Yes ma'am.'

As she walked up to the entrance he saw her do a double-take, her attention focused on the road and a bright red and black Ford 4x4. He watched, as her gaze followed the vehicle past the front of the hotel. As she went inside he too looked across the road, with enough time to see the Ford disappear around the corner but not before noticing the man in the driving seat was wearing dark glasses and a baseball cap.

The foyer was filling up with the wives, sisters and daughters of the most powerful men in the land. The women behind the senators, congressmen and diplomats chatted and mingled together with owners and CEO's of major domestic and international companies but the real power was with the handful of women who were the direct descendants of the Pilgrim Fathers. These women were more than the social elite; they were the most influential women in the country.

As she smiled and eased her way deeper into the foyer, Lisa saw Emily Harding-West waving discretely from the entrance to the dining room.

The dining room was set with over thirty round tables, each with ten place-settings. The perfume of fresh spring flowers permeated the air and a classical harpist played Debussy from the small stage in the corner, the haunting lullaby echoing around the great hall.

After cheeks were kissed and hugs exchanged, Lisa and Emily made their way to the table.

'Thank you so much, Emily for getting me in here today. And again I'm sorry for calling so late last night.'

'Oh, darling don't be silly. Although it did raise the question from James, as to why I was taking calls in the middle of the night.'

Lisa frowned. 'Oh, I'm so sorry.'

Emily laughed lightly and shrugged her shoulders. 'I told him it was my lover.'

Lisa laughed. 'Really? You didn't?'

'I did.'

'What did he say?

'He just rolled over and said, then please ask him to call at a more respectable time in future.'

More laughter from them both and Lisa said, 'So what did you say?'

'I said, what makes you think it's a man?'

'Oh, Emily, you really do get worse, honey.'

The socialite pursed her lips. 'If only I could. Ah, here we are, here's our table, darling.'

As they took their seats, Lisa leaned in close and said, 'There are a couple more big favours I need to ask, Emily.'

'Ooh, this is very mysterious, darling. Almost exciting. What?'

'Could you get me two tickets to the Inauguration Ball, please?'

Emily frowned. 'Is that all? It's a little a little late but James has two tables reserved. I'll get him to put your names on our VIP guest list and you can sit with us. Who's your plus-one darling?'

'Mr Jack Castle.'

Emily leaned in even closer. 'That's a name I've not heard before. A new lover?'

'Emily Harding-West, you are incorrigible. He's just a very good friend from England.'

'Oh, daring, I simply love Englishmen. And the other?'

'Other what?' said Lisa.'

'You said two favours, darling.'

Lisa looked around and then spoke very quietly. 'Ah yes and this is the most important. Before we leave today, I need you to introduce me to the Vice President Elect's wife.'

'Of course, darling. That won't be a problem. I was good friends with her daughter, Samantha.'

Lisa frowned. 'Was?'

'Yes, was unfortunately. She was such a wonderful girl. Such a waste. Killed on active service.'

Chapter Thirty Four
'The Helen & Chuck Meeting'

Across the city at 950 Pennsylvania Avenue, a meeting was about to take place in the Robert Kennedy Department of Justice Building, between the Attorney General and the Director of the FBI.

The Attorney General is the most senior law enforcement officer in America. The Director of the Federal Bureau of Investigation is the most senior domestic investigator and both of these prestigious appointments are bestowed by the President.

Helen Masterson, the current AG had been in the role for almost eight years and was keen to remain in the position when the new President took office. Indeed it was vital to her to ensure she remained the incumbent, as her ambitions of a seat in Congress depended on it.

Charles 'Chuck' Gresham, the Director of the FBI had been in his role for a little over four years and he too had the desire to stay in office after the forthcoming inauguration.

Earlier that day, Helen Masterson had received a sealed case via secure messenger from the FBI. The mere fact this information had been sent in this manner set off alarms bells in Masterson's head. On the case were the words ATTORNEY GENERAL EYES ONLY and only the most secret and sensitive information was passed in this manner. She had signed for the case and later, alone in her office, had gone through the dossier of evidence Jack Castle had passed to the NSA and FBI. She'd also read through the FBI director's report.

It was a little after two o'clock when Chuck Gresham entered her office. It was well known throughout the security and law fraternity that these two top individuals did not like each other. Gresham felt the AG interfered too much with his department's modus operandi and Masterson felt the director's methods bordered on the cavalier. Never-the-less, both being political animals and both being of a mind to progress up the Washington diplomatic ladder, understood the need to work together when certain events presented themselves. This case was one of those times.

The AG stood as the FBI director entered her office. 'Chuck. Good to see you again.'

'You too, Helen.'

'Have a seat. Can I get you anything to drink?'

He raised his hand. 'I'm fine for now. Thank you.'

She sat down and laid her hand on the small pile of documents in front of her. 'Powerful stuff, Chuck.'

The director nodded soberly. 'What are we going to do, Helen? How do you want to work this?'

'Tell me how you came to get hold of this information, Chuck.'

The director waved his hand. It's all in my report.'

'Yes, I've read that. But tell me about this Brit, Jack Castle. Is he to be trusted, reliable?'

Gresham shifted in his seat. 'He's a very successful businessman, operates a respected international security

151

company. Our Department of Defence has contracts with him in Iraq and Afghanistan.'

'I think he's a bit more than a business man, Chuck?'

'Think I will have a drink. Maybe some water please?'

She pressed a button on the intercom. 'Michael, can we get a bottle of water, please and bring me a coffee. Go on, Chuck.'

'Jack Castle is ex British special forces. The SAS. He's a very capable man.'

Masterson smiled and nodded slightly. 'The British bulldog, eh?'

The knock on the door was answered with a, 'Come in,' from Masterson.

The aide put a tray on the corner of the desk. 'Okay Michael, that's fine. Thank you.'

Gresham picked up the water, cracked the cap and drank from the bottle, bringing a frown to the elegant woman's face.

'Please, go on, Chuck.'

'After getting the original information from his dying buddy Charles Webster, he flew to Afghanistan. He contacted another of his old friends in Kabul, who confirmed an unscheduled flight did go to Russia, allegedly with the stolen opium.'

The AG sipped at her coffee. 'This man Castle seems to have a lot of friends?'

'You have no idea. He has contacts all over the world, especially in Russia.'

'Should we be worried about that?' said Masterson.

'I don't think so. This guy is true British through and through. His Russian contacts usually come via his father-in-law, Dimitri Orlov.'

Masterson put her cup down. 'Not the Russian billionaire?'

'The very same. Castle married his daughter a couple of years ago.'

The AG smiled. 'Married into money eh?'

'Not really. They were together for almost fifteen years before they married. Castle is a multimillionaire in his own right. They have a couple of children now.'

She tapped the pile of documents. 'So why's he chasing around the world getting involved with this kind of thing?'

Gresham shrugged his shoulders. 'I guess he's 'boy scout' and always wants to do the right thing. Maybe an action junkie. Who knows?'

The AG took another sip of coffee. 'We're getting off the subject. Carry on, Chuck.'

'So he goes from Afghanistan to Moscow and meets up with another old friend who puts him in contact with a big Moscow mafia boss, Alexei Kuragin. It was his family who allegedly bought the opium.'

Masterson stood up and walked to the window. 'Any relation to the Kuragin crime family in New York?'

Gresham nodded. 'They were brothers.'

'Christ, this gets worse,' said the AG. 'Go on, Chuck.'

'Castle then comes to Washington and meets up with Lisa Reynard.'

'She's the journalist, working with the NSA?' said Masterson.

'That's correct.'

The AG took a deep breath. 'And of course Mr Castle knew she was NSA?'

Gresham nodded. 'Yes of course. They actually worked together about a year ago.'

She turned from the window. 'What?'

'Yes, they worked together on the Vinnie Shahadi operation. It was Jack Castle and a couple of his friends who captured the arms dealer and got him back to London. Castle saved Reynard's life after she'd been shot in Moscow.'

'So Jack Castle is really MI6?'

'He was then but I spoke to London and they categorically deny he is on mission for them now.'

The AG smiled. 'That means he's independent but working with their knowledge.'

She turned back to the window and watched a small skene of ducks as it flew across the sky. 'So Castle and Reynard tracked down this Colonel Nelson and handed him over to you?'

'That's right.'

Masterson turned around. 'And Colonel Nelson is now dead.'

Gresham fiddled with the water bottle and said, 'Yeah, along with my deputy and six of our agents.'

The AG resumed her seat behind the desk. 'The body count is rising by the day, Chuck. Just how many is that now?'

Gresham looked uncomfortable. 'Four aircrew killed when the plane was shot down in Afghanistan. Eight alleged conspirators, plus three collateral deaths. My deputy and six agents, makes twenty two. We don't really know how many died in the attack on the Kuragin dacha in Russia.'

The AG shook her head slightly. 'Christ, what a fucking mess.'

Gresham had never heard the woman swear before. Masterson leaned forward and laid both hands on the pile of documents. 'And this is the evidence which allegedly points to our President Elect being responsible?'

'That's right, Helen.'

Chapter Thirty Five
'The Creepy Guy'

The *Mayflower* lunch had finished a little after five o'clock. Thanks to the introduction from Emily Harding-West, Lisa had spoken to the Vice President Elect's wife and was able to pass on the flash-disc Jack had prepared. It was a little before six when Lisa and Jack drove into the basement parking of Lisa's building and were surprised to find a van parked in Lisa's bay.

'Aww, look at this,' she said.

'The engine's running,' said Jack. 'I'll ask the driver to move.'

Jack got out and shouted towards the van but there was no response. He walked over and around to the driver's side out of sight. Lisa waited several seconds but he didn't come back. She beeped the horn a couple of times but still no sign of Jack or the driver. She was about to get out when her passenger door was pulled open and a man leaned in, a large revolver in his hand.

'Step out of the car. And don't try anything stupid or your boyfriend is dead.'

She climbed out and shouted, 'What the hell is this?'

'Just do as you're told, lady. Over to the van.'

When Lisa turned the corner of the van she saw Jack on the floor. Immediately she tried to kneel down, but the man with the gun pulled her to her feet.

'Don't worry, he's alive. Now up against the van. Move, lady.'

A second man had secured Jack's hands with cable ties and was hauling him into the open side door of the vehicle. The gunman quickly searched Lisa, the muzzle of the weapon pressed hard between her shoulder blades.

'Hands behind your back.'

She felt the plastic ties pulled tight around her wrists.

'Now get in.'

She climbed in and took a seat on a worn leather bench. Jack was bundled onto the floor at her feet. She could see the hair at the back of his head was matted with blood. As the door was slammed shut he rolled over. His eyes slowly opened. She leaned forward unable to help him but said quietly, 'You okay, Jack?'

He took a breath and let out a deep moan. 'Fuck. I walked right into that. Yes, I'm okay, apart from a bloody headache and a severely wounded ego.'

'Always the joker, eh, Jack?'

As the vehicle reversed out of the bay, Jack said, 'I doubt I can make these jokers laugh.'

Through the dirty windscreen Lisa saw the second man drive her Porsche into the parking bay, lock the vehicle and then climb into the back of the van. He took a seat alongside Lisa, the revolver in hand. 'Just relax and enjoy the ride.'

A little over an hour later the van came to a stop. Jack heard the kidnappers talking but couldn't make out what was being said. The van door was pulled open and the bright evening sunlight blinded them for a moment or two.

'Okay, out.'

Jack shuffled across the floor and sat on the threshold for a few seconds quickly scanning the surrounding area. They were in the country in what appeared to be a deserted farm or ranch.

'Get your ass up.'

Jack stood and waited as Lisa was helped down. He thought of attacking the men but, with hands tied and two men to take on, it would be fruitless.

'Okay, this way.'

They were taken over to a derelict barn and, as the door was pulled open, a third, and decidedly creepy older man appeared.

'Okay, boys. I'll take it from here. You can go.'

One of the kidnappers cut the ties on Jack and Lisa's hands then pushed them forward. The creepy guy produced a nine-mill automatic and cocked the weapon.

'You sure you don't want us to stay?'

The creepy guy smiled, showing several broken teeth. 'Oh, no. I can manage this. I'll call you when I need you.'

'You're the boss.'

Jack watched the two return to the van and drive off. The dust cloud from the spinning tyres blew past and caused the creep to cough, Jack smiled at his discomfort. The man waved the big automatic towards the interior of the building. 'Inside please.'

The room was dirty and damp, with a faint smell of urine. Daylight came in from a single barred window high up on the wall. In one corner was an old metal desk, a battered and torn leather chair behind it. In the other corner stood a small table with an array of objects laid out on the rusty metal top; a metal bar, two thick whips, several knives of various sizes and a dirty wooden baseball bat. A metal chair was on its side on the floor. Two chains hung from a pipe in the ceiling and below several heavy duty eyelets, drilled into the concrete.

'Oh, shit,' said Lisa.

The creep smiled at her reaction. 'I see you like my little office.'

'You sick fuck,' said Jack.

The man smiled at the insult. 'Please, let's keep this civilised.'

Lisa turned. 'Civilised?'

The man kept the gun on Jack. With the other hand he pointed to the area under the hanging chains. 'Over there, please.'

They moved slowly to the centre of the room and turned to face the creepy gunman.

'What now?' said Jack.

The man smiled again, his eyes widened. 'Now, please undress.'

'Fuck you.' spat Lisa.

Jack turned and looked into her eyes, then began to remove his clothes.

'Thank you,' said the creep, still smiling.

Their captor moved to the old desk and sat down behind it. He watched as Lisa stripped down to her underwear. His face changed. 'Everything. All off please.'

As they removed their underwear, they heard a metal drawer screech open. The man took something from the drawer and threw it over towards them. 'Put them on his wrists and ankles, please.'

159

Lisa picked up the shackles and strapped them on Jack.

The man stood up. 'Arms up, please. Clip him to the chain.'

The chain rattled as she attached his wrists.

He waved the gun. 'The feet as well, please.'

Jack spread his legs and Lisa looked up into his face as she attached his ankles to the floor.

Their captor smiled. 'Thank you, my dear. Now please attach the restraints to your own ankles and wrists.'

She did as he said then stood defiant, the fear gone, replaced by anger.

He walked behind her and placed the muzzle of the gun gently against her spine. 'Arms up, please, my dear.'

Then kneeling, he secured one leg to the floor; Lisa shuddered, as his cheek inadvertently touched the back of her thigh. The last manacle was secured and he stood in front of them. Smiling, he turned away and moved to the table, picked up one of the whips, and returned to Lisa. He ran the flail down her hip, his eyes on the curve of her body, then recoiled as she spat in his face. He stood back, the smile ever present. He wiped the spittle from his face and licked his finger. 'Perhaps we'll get to this a little later.' He bent down and collected their clothes then spread them out the rusty desk top. After methodically going through all the pockets he ended up with a small pile of their personal effects. Smiling at his two captives he said, 'Now let's see who we have here?'

'Fuck you,' said Jack.

The creep had Jack's passport and was flicking through the pages. 'Mr Jack Castle, a British businessman.' He looked at Jack. 'I don't think so.'

Jack looked him straight in the eyes. 'Like I said. Fuck you.'

He picked up Lisa pocketbook and took out her driver's licence and Washington Post ID card. 'Miss Lisa Reynard, journalist.' He looked at her, his eyes moving up and down her naked body. 'And what else are you, Miss Reynard? Not just a journalist?'

She narrowed her eyes. 'Like Jack said, shit-head. Fuck you.'

He left the desk and walked over to her, the whip in his hand. Again he ran the flail across her stomach tracing the gunshot scar. 'I see you are no stranger to pain, Miss Reynard.'

'Leave her alone,' said Jack.

The creep turned to Jack. 'For now, I shall leave you both alone to consider your position. All I need to know is everything you know.' Still smiling, he walked to the door, then turned. 'Your fates are solely dependent on your cooperation.'

The door creaked shut behind him.

Lisa looked at Jack and saw the smile. 'What the hell have you got to smile about?'

He grinned. 'In any other circumstances seeing you like this might have been fun.'

She shook her head. 'Another time, another place maybe. If we survive this, that is.'

'We'll survive. This fucker's not going to do anything here. He's not going to torture us at least.'

'And how d'you figure that?'

'Look at the restraints. They're brand new and padded. He could have used cable ties, rope, or those shackles over there. These have been used so as not to leave marks. Which means he, or whoever he's working for, does not want any evidence on our bodies. All this is a bluff. If we talk he gets what he wants and will kill us elsewhere, make it look like an accident. If we don't talk, the outcome will be the same. Whatever happens we're not gonna die here.'

She looked into his eyes. 'Jesus, Jack. I hope you're right.'

Chapter Thirty Six
'The Baby's Egg'

The sun was setting over The Magnolia Estate, its golden rays turning the façade of the big house from white to soft amber. On the west patio, President Elect Alex Mason and Senator David Ashton were enjoying their mint juleps.

Alex Mason laid his hand on the blue velvet bag. 'Well, Senator. I have to say this is a wonderful gift. Where on earth did you manage to find it.'

The senator smiled. 'Oh, I have my sources, sir. Let's just say, when I saw it I knew you would appreciate it.'

'It is very generous indeed and certainly exquisite.'

The senator drained his julep and said, 'You are very welcome, sir. I'm pleased you like it.'

Mason nodded and smiled. 'How was that julep, David? Tart enough for you?'

'Perfect, sir, just perfect.'

'Care for another?'

The senator smiled and raised his glass, relieved the gift had not exploded, 'Why not, sir?'

Mason picked up a small silver bell from the table and shook it. A few seconds later the butler appeared. 'Sir?'

'Two more please, Henry?'

Elizabeth Rhodes-Mason came out of the house. 'Make that three, please, Henry.'

The butler bowed his head slightly. 'Certainly, madam.'

Taking a seat next to her husband, she said, 'And what are you two boys talking about?' She noticed the blue bag and continued. 'And what's this?'

Mason smiled and picked up the bag. 'It's a gift from the senator here.'

He unfastened the draw string and removed a highly polished mahogany case about the size of a shoe box. On the lid, and set in gold relief, was a magnificent depiction of a two headed eagle, its wings spread wide. Above the twin heads was a crown, in one claw a sceptre, in the other an orb. Below the creature was one word in Russian Cyrillic, ROMANOV. He opened the case to reveal a fitted interior, finished in royal blue satin. Inside the lid was an embossed copper-plate certificate, which read . . .

SOTHEBY & Co. LONDON

In the spring of 1866 Tsar Alexander III's wife, Maria Fedorovna, miscarried her first baby.
In an attempt to console his broken hearted wife and in memory of their lost child, the Tsar commissioned Peter Carl Fabergé to produce this commemorative egg.
'The Baby's Egg' as it came to be known, was lost until 1991, at which time it came onto the market and was sold by Sotheby & Co. London.

Charles Henry Mortimer.
Appraisals Director.
Sotheby & Co. London.

Elizabeth Mason gasped when she saw the magnificently jewelled egg. 'Oh, my god. That is the most beautiful thing I have ever seen.'

Her husband picked up the artefact and turned it around in his hands, admiring the beautiful enamel work and gem encrusted shell.

'It is absolutely exquisite,' said Mason. He was about to hand it to his wife when he noticed the smallest of hinges at the circumference. 'What's this?'

On the opposite side to the hinge was a tiny, almost concealed, button. Intrigued, he gently pressed the miniscule switch and the egg clicked silently open.

'Ooh,' he said as he looked at his thumb.

'What?' said Elizabeth.'

A tiny spec appeared on the thumb. He sucked off the dot of blood. 'It's nothing,' he said and opened the egg to reveal a perfect miniature of a winged cherub, made of solid gold.

'Would you look at that? Quite amazing,' said, the President Elect.

The butler returning with the drinks broke the moment.

'Ah, juleps,' said Elizabeth.

Mason closed up the egg and returned it lovingly to its case, then placed the case inside the velvet bag.

As he picked up his glass he saw the tiny spec of blood again. Rubbing his finger and thumb, it disappeared. He raised the julep and said, 'Yes indeed, Senator. That is quite a gift.'

Chapter Thirty Seven
'Let the Bastard Rot'

Lisa and Jack had been alone for almost twenty minutes when they were startled by the sound of gun shots outside.

'What fresh hell is this?' said Lisa.

Jack grinned for a second at the Shakespearian quote. 'Let's hope it's not more bad news.'

The door slowly opened and the last rays of the evening sun blinded them for a few seconds. Then, as the door was pulled fully open it silhouetted the figure of a large man. As he stepped into the room a second figure appeared in the doorway. Lisa's eyes adjusted to the brightness and she saw it was the man in the baseball cap and sunglass. The larger of the two men approached and stood, hands on his hips, in front of them. 'What the fuck you been up to boss?' said Grigory Markov.

The second man approached, removed the cap and glasses. 'Hello, Lisa,' he said.

Her mouth hung open for a few seconds. 'Tom Hillman?'

Jack and Lisa were quickly freed from the restraints. After getting dressed and collecting their personal effects, they left the building. The blood covered body of the creepy guy was laid out in the dirt, a few yards away from the building. Grigory had set off down the road to recover their hidden vehicle and as the sun was setting over the deserted ranch Lisa turned to Jack and punched him hard on the upper arm. 'You bastard, Castle. You knew we had backup all the time.'

'Ooh, that's bloody sore,' said Jack as he rubbed his arm.

She raised her fist again but Jack quickly backed away. He and Tom laughed.

'Calm down, babe,' said Jack.

'Why wouldn't you tell me?' said Lisa, clearly annoyed.

'I didn't want to have to get the guys involved unless it was absolutely necessary.'

'But you still could have told me, Jack. I saw Tom a couple of times and thought we were being followed.'

'I guess I should have, but I didn't. Sorry, babe.'

Grigory's arrival in a red and black Ford 4x4 made her smile.

Nodding towards the body of the creep, Tom said, 'What you want to do about this fucker?'

Jack climbed into the truck. 'Let the bastard rot.'

Grigory pulled off the deserted ranch road and onto the main road just as it was getting dark. Tom leaned over the back seat and took out two bottles of water, then handed them to Lisa and Jack.

'I could do with something a little stronger than this,' said Lisa.

'Me too,' said Jack, as he glugged the refreshing liquid down.

'Thought you didn't drink boss?' said Markov.

'I could make an exception right now, buddy.'

They all laughed.

Lisa rubbed her wrists and then leaned forward over the seat. She held her hand out to Grigory and said, 'We haven't been introduced yet. I'm Lisa Reynard.'

The big Russian smiled and shook hands. 'Grigory Vasilyevich Markov.'

'Thank you for rescuing me, Grigory.'

'Was my pleasure, Miss Lisa. Is first time I rescue naked lady.'

They all laughed again.

Lisa finished her water. 'So when did you guys get here?'

'I flew in from Dubai the day before Jack arrived from Moscow. Grigory came in on the same flight as Vanya Kuragin,' said Tom.

'Da, I travel cattle class. Vanya never sees me.'

Lisa nodded. 'And you two guys have never met before?'

Markov looked over his shoulder. 'No. But these are great friends of my brother Bogdan. So now are my friends also. If they need help. I help.'

'So I guess it was you two who Marcus Nelson spotted following Jack from the airport?'

'Maybe,' said Tom.

'Or maybe the bastards who picked us up today,' said Jack.

'Where have you guys been staying?' said Lisa.

'Small hotels,' said Tom. 'Different one each night, pay cash, negative foot-print.'

Lisa leaned across and gave Tom a kiss on the cheek. 'Once a spook always a spook, eh?'

They all laughed.

As they drove through the darkness, Grigory said, 'What's the plan now, boss?'

In the front passenger seat Jack turned to face his three companions. 'The inauguration is the day after tomorrow. The FBI has all the evidence and now, thanks to Lisa, so should the Vice President Elect. I guess we see how the next few days pan out and sit tight.'

'You're right. There isn't much more we can do,' said Tom.

'So we go off the radar and lie low for a couple of days?' said Lisa.

Jack nodded. 'Yeah, which means we don't go back to your apartment.'

'Okay, then how about my place in the country?'

Jack turned back and watched the road. 'Yeah, sounds good. Where are we now Grigory?'

'We about three miles from Highway 66, east of Washington.'

'Okay,' said Lisa. 'Soon as you hit the main highway turn south. Follow the signs for Branton. My house is in a little village just outside. We should be there in about an hour.'

Jack looked over his shoulder and smiled at her. 'Looks like you got a couple more house guests, babe.'

'That's okay, the freezer's full.'

'As long as beer fridge is full,' said Grigory.'

They all laughed.

Jack finished off his water. 'What weapons do we have, Tom?'

'Grigory and I have a nine-mill each. And a dozen clips.'

'I have a Glock, a shotgun and a hunting rifle at the house,' added Lisa.

Jack turned around, a bemused look on his face.

'What?' said Lisa. 'Coz I'm a girl I'm not allowed to have guns?'

They all laughed again.

Chapter Thirty Eight
'Morning'

The following morning, the weather in Washington was overcast but warm. The dull clouds were clearing, thanks to a light breeze coming in from the west and the day promised to be a pleasant one. That, of course, was only as far as the meteorologists were concerned.

On the roof of The J. Edgar Hoover building, FBI Director Chuck Gresham and Attorney General Helen Masterson waited to be called forward to the helicopter. The flight would take them down to *The Magnolia Estate* and their meeting with President Elect Alex Mason. Neither felt particularly comfortable about the questions they would have to ask their new boss. Nevertheless, a major crime had been perpetrated, multiple murders committed, and a huge conspiracy was evident. In normal circumstances anyone involved, or even thought to be involved would have been swiftly arrested and subject to the most stringent questioning. Unfortunately, with the future president implicated, this case was anything but normal and both Masterson and Gresham felt the outcome of today's meeting could cost them their careers. Or, should the case develop and Alex Mason found to be involved and ultimately guilty, they would be the two people who brought a president to justice.

* * *

Jack, Lisa, Tom and Grigory, had arrived at her country house a little after eight the previous evening. Lisa was pretty sure their arrival went un-noticed by any of the neighbours from the other half dozen houses in the select and decidedly upmarket hamlet. The big 4x4 had been concealed in the garage and the four of them kept to the rear of the property, with no lights showing at the front. To anyone passing, the house still looked empty.

During the night they'd taken it in turn to stand watch and by seven o'clock the next morning were all in the big kitchen eating a welcome breakfast, expertly cooked by Grigory.

'That pool looks inviting,' said Jack. 'Shame we need to lie low. Looks like it's gonna be a nice day as well, once the cloud clears.'

'Da,' said the big Russian, as he piled more scrambled eggs onto his plate. 'I don't have swim for long time.'

'Did you get any sleep, Jack?' said Tom.

'Nah, just a couple of hours.'

Lisa switched on the big wall mounted TV and flicked through the channels to CNN's Washington news. The screen was flooded by a wide angle shot of the Capitol Building and the preparations for the following day's inauguration. She flicked to a couple of other news channels; all basically reported on the next day's events. There was nothing about Alex Mason's involvement in the Afghan conspiracy.

'Looks like the Vice President Elect hasn't acted on the information we gave him,' said Lisa.

Jack stood up and went to the window. 'There's still over twenty four hours before he's sworn in. The FBI has got to do something. They can't just sit on the evidence. And don't forget all the killings. Even if they're sceptical about the documented evidence, they're duty bound to look more closely at the murders, especially as their own Deputy Director has been killed. Let's see how the next day or two pans out.'

Tom poured himself another mug of coffee. 'Just because he gets sworn-in and becomes President doesn't mean he can't still be arrested and questioned. He's not immune.'

'That's right, Tom,' said Lisa. 'So we wait and see what happens over the next coupla days.'

* * *

The flight from Washington was comfortable. Chuck Gresham and Helen Masterson viewed the city and surrounding countryside from their respective sides of the helicopter. The Attorney General never enjoyed helicopter flights but Gresham loved the idea of having an FBI chopper at his beck-and-call. He'd miss this perk if the coming meeting's events went wrong and he was out of a job. Both were absorbed with their own thoughts of how today would develop and they barely spoke a dozen words to each other on the twenty-five minute journey down to *The Magnolia Estate*.

Helen Masterson was not happy about having to confront The President Elect; that was Gresham's job. The FBI or the police were responsible for acting on information and evidence and only the FBI or police usually arrested a suspect, but Gresham had made a compelling case for her to attend the interview with him.

Gresham, of course, had insisted Masterson supported him during the meeting for no other reason than self-preservation. If it all went wrong then Mason's wrath would fall on both of them, not just him. Alternatively, if it did become evident Alex Mason was indeed implicated, then the glory would unfortunately be shared. It was a 'win-no-win' situation and, at this moment in time, the outcome was definitely uncertain.

Their thoughts were disturbed by the pilot's voice coming over the speaker. 'Good morning again, sir, ma'am. Landing in two minutes. Please ensure your seat belts are secure.'

Chapter Thirty Nine
'A Commanding Position'

President Elect Alex Mason was eating breakfast on the east patio. The smell of jasmine, so prevalent in the evening had dissipated. The clouds had cleared and the warm sun on Mason's back felt good, even though he'd felt under the weather for the last couple of days.

He didn't bother to stand when his visitors were shown onto the patio by the butler.

'Mrs Masterson and Mr Gresham, sir,'

Mason smiled at the introduction, the butler clearly following his order not to use their official titles.

'Thank you, Henry. Helen, Chuck, good to see you again. Please have a seat. Can we get you some breakfast?'

'Nothing for me, sir,' said Gresham, as he took a seat on the opposite side of the table.

Masterson turned to the butler. 'I'd love some coffee, please.'

With mild satisfaction the President Elect noted the two's discomfort. He'd purposefully sat with his back to the sun, thus ensuring his visitors would be facing directly into it. Their attempts to subtly manoeuvre their chairs out of the almost blinding sunlight made him smile. *Always take a commanding position*, he thought.

'Thank you for seeing us, sir,' said the FBI director. 'We know how busy you must be at this time.'

'Yes, indeed, thank you, sir,' added Helen Masterson.

With a slight wave of his hand Mason said, 'Oh, I'm not that busy and I always have time to talk to the Director of the FBI and the Attorney General.' He smiled, picked up a large crystal tumbler of orange juice and took a drink, wiped his lips with a crisp linen napkin and said, 'So what's so important to bring you both down here today?'

Chuck Gresham cleared his throat. 'You were in Afghanistan in 2005, sir.'

Mason nodded slightly. 'I was.'

'There was a cargo plane shot down, allegedly loaded with over seventy tons of captured Taliban opium.'

The President Elect took a sip from a china coffee cup, then looked across the table. 'I remember it well, Chuck. Four aircrew died that day.'

Gresham shuffled in his chair, the sun uncomfortable in his eyes. 'We have evidence, sir that the plane which was destroyed was not actually carrying any opium.'

Mason leaned back, removed the napkin from his lap and placed it on the table. 'Evidence?'

'Yes, sir.'

'So you are looking into the so called disappearance of this opium?'

'Yes, sir. That and other issues.'

Mason narrowed his eyes. 'Surely this must be a matter for the Military to deal with, Chuck?'

'If it was only the disappearance of the opium, sir, I would agree. But there seems to be a conspiracy to steal the cargo.'

'Really?' said Mason, a look of surprise on his face. 'But it should still be a Military matter.'

Gresham continued to shuffle in his chair. 'May I have some water please?'

Mason rang a small silver bell. A few seconds later the butler appeared. 'Some water please, Henry,' said Mason, then turned back to Gresham. 'You were saying, Chuck?'

'Yes, sir. Not only is there evidence of a conspiracy to steal the opium but, it would appear, anyone who had anything to do with the theft has been murdered, here in America and in Russia.'

Alex Mason pushed his chair back from the table. 'Russia?'

'Yes, sir. The evidence points to the cargo being sold to the Moscow Mafia.'

'This all sounds rather fanciful, Chuck.'

The water arrived and Gresham swallowed almost a full glass before speaking again. 'There have been several murders of high ranking officers, sir. All of which appear to be involved in the conspiracy.'

'American officers?' said Mason.

'Yes, sir.'

Mason turned to the Attorney General. 'And what do you make of all this, Helen?'

Masterson was clearly uncomfortable being asked a direct question. 'The documented evidence and the murders all tie-in, sir. The evidence we have is indeed compelling.'

The President Elect stood up, casting a shadow over the couple opposite. 'Documented evidence?'

'Yes, sir,' said Gresham,' pleased to have a little respite from the direct sunlight. 'We have names, dates and copies of orders. Information on where the stolen cargo went to in Russia and Cayman bank accounts showing where the mafia sent the payments. We also have a video statement from one of the conspirators before he was killed.'

Mason moved away from the table and the sunlight hit the couple again. 'This is amazing, Chuck and it seems like you have done a great job in discovering all this information. But if, as you indicate, the conspirators are all dead then who do you plan to bring to justice?'

Gresham and Masterson stood up. 'We'll still be looking for whoever has been involved with the murders, sir,' said the FBI director.

Mason smiled. 'And I'm sure the FBI will be successful in its endeavours, Chuck, but I don't see why you needed to bring this to me?'

Gresham shuffled slightly, clearly very uncomfortable with the whole conversation. 'The evidence, sir, points to one person masterminding the conspiracy.'

'And do you know who that person is?' said Mason.

Gresham stood silent, he could feel himself trembling.

'Well, Chuck?'

The director cleared his throat, stood upright and looked directly at Mason. 'The evidence points to you, sir.'

The President Elect's eyes narrowed to dark slits. He looked at Gresham, then Masterson, then threw his head back and laughed out loud.

Chapter Forty
'Hello Again, Hun'

The last thirty six hours at Lisa's country house had been uneventful. They'd each taken their turn to stand watch on both nights and it was clear whoever had been after them were not yet aware of their current location. Jack had just finished his watch when he heard someone in the kitchen. Lisa was making coffee when he entered, sawn-off shotgun under his arm. The smell of bacon permeated the air.

'Well, that bastard gets sworn in today,' he said.

She turned and looked sternly at him. 'And a good morning to you too, Mr Castle.'

'Sorry, babe. Good morning.'

'You want some breakfast, hun?'

'Tea and a bacon sandwich would be great.'

She frowned at him as he laid her mutilated shotgun on the counter. 'You've made a right mess of that gun.'

He picked up the weapon and smiled sheepishly. Most of the stock had been cut off and the double barrels had been sawn down to a third of their original length. 'I'll get you a new one when this is all over, sweetie. Even send you to Italy to get it fitted properly.'

She took the bacon from under the grill. 'Yeah, I'll believe that when I see it.'

The big TV on the wall was silent but showed images of the Capitol Building. A huge stage had been built on the front steps. Red, white and blue banners hung everywhere and a massive Stars and Stripes festooned the front of the imposing edifice. The screen-shot then panned to reveal the already gathering crowds.

'Christ, look at that,' said Jack. 'There's thousands there already and it's only six o'clock.'

Tom entered. 'You Yanks love a parade.'

Jack chuckled. 'Don't they just.'

'You two want to get your own breakfasts then?' said Lisa with feigned indignation.

Grigory came in. 'I love Americans. They always spend plenty in my restaurant.'

The men laughed and Lisa shook her head.

As they sat around the big breakfast bar, Tom said, 'What time are we heading back to DC?'

Jack looked at his Rolex, it was almost six fifteen. 'We should leave about seven-thirty, right Lisa?'

'Yeah. Usually takes about an hour to get back to the apartment from here. Probably be a lot longer today though, the roads are gonna be busy with inauguration crowds.'

'Okay,' said Jack. 'Let's eat, then get ready to leave.'

The day a president is inaugurated is not a public holiday and although most people should be working, not many actually do. Those who don't get to join the massed crowds in front of the Capitol Building watch the ceremony on TV but it still means the streets and traffic around the city are decidedly busier than normal.

It was almost nine o'clock when the Ford stopped just before Dupont Circle. Lisa had been right and the journey had taken almost half as long again. Jack and

Lisa got out and waved to several taxis before one finally stopped and picked them up.

'Connecticut Avenue, please. North end,' said Lisa as she climbed in.

The Yellow Cab eased away from the sidewalk. In the 4x4, Grigory gunned the engine and almost knocked over a cyclist as he forced the big truck into the busy steam of traffic. He smiled as he looked in the rear view mirror, the irate cyclist shaking his fist and then raising a middle finger. Another dangerous manoeuvre and he was in front of a small delivery van. Several beeps on the horn from yet another unhappy road-user made him smile again. He settled into the fast moving stream and followed Jack's taxi, now only two cars in front.

On Connecticut Avenue the traffic heading into the city was congested, but Northbound carriageway moved swiftly so it took less than ten minutes to get from Dupont Circle to Lisa's apartment block. The taxi pulled off the road into the short driveway and up to the front of the stylish building. Jack paid the driver and watched as he drove off. They entered the foyer and were greeted by the old concierge. 'Good morning, Miss Reynard.'

Lisa smiled and walked over to the desk. 'Morning, Gary. How are you today?'

'I'm good, miss. Looking forward to the ceremony. You know, I served with the President back in Saigon.'

Lisa continued to smile. 'Really? You must be very proud, Gary. Any post and deliveries for me?'

'Yes ma'am. Hold on one minute please.'

Jack watched as the old guy went into the back office, coming out a few seconds later with a small pile of envelopes and a large flat reinforced cardboard box. 'There you are, miss.'

'Thanks, Gary. There's just one other thing I'm afraid. I seem to have left my keys at the office. Would you mind asking the Superintendent if he can come up and let me in please?'

'Of course, miss.'

'Thanks, Gary. See you later.'

Lisa collected the envelopes and Jack picked up the big box. He smiled as he read the bold lettering, *Calvini. Formal Dress Hire.* As they waited for the lift they heard Gary talking to the superintendent.

By the time they got to her apartment door the superintendent was already waiting for them. Lisa shook her head. 'How did you manage to get up here before us, George?'

George smiled. 'I was on the floor above, miss.'

The door was unlocked and Jack went inside. Lisa spent a second or two talking to George and then followed. She put the envelopes down on the hall stand and went into the sitting room. Jack was standing with his back to her. The box still in his hands.

'What you doing, hun?'

Jack stepped aside and Lisa saw the man sitting in the big armchair, feet up on the footstool, a silenced Smith and Wesson pointing straight at Jack. The gunman smiled and said, 'Hello again, hun.'

Jack recognised him as one of the men who'd taken them two days ago. This time he was alone and Jack was not tied up. Jack's brain was racing. The man was seated, feet up, definitely an easy opponent in that position. The weapon was a problem, but there were

182

only ten feet between him and the gunman. *Throw the box, step to the side, dive on the bastard.* Jack was about to make the move when a second man's voice behind him said. 'Don't go trying any hero type shit, Limey.'

The seated man stood and walked towards Jack, a slight smirk on his lips. 'I don't know how you managed to get away from that barn, buddy. But it aint gonna happen again.' The smirk turned to a sneer and the man's eyes narrowed. 'If it were up to me, I'd put a bullet in both your heads right here.' He waved the gun at Lisa. 'But there are people who want you two to just vanish.'

'Yeah,' said the second man. 'And this time you're gonna stay vanished. We're gonna take the elevator down to the parking garage and we're goin on a little ride. Now move your fuckin asses.'

They left the apartment and walked towards the lifts. At the end of the corridor was a small seating area. A rather large jolly looking man was sitting reading one of the glossy magazines. He looked over the top of the journal and smiled pleasantly as the group approached. The first gunman pressed the button and all four looked up at the lights of the floor indicator.

The second gunman did not know what hit him. Grigory's Glock smashed into the back of his head rendering him unconscious before he hit the floor. The first man turned swiftly to find the big Russian's gun pointing at his head.

Jack took hold of the gunman's arm and slowly eased it out of his pocket. 'Nice and easy arsehole.' He took the revolver from the man's hand and then head-butted him hard in the face. The gunman fell back against the lift door, moaning, blood streaming from his nose.

'That's for the lump on my head.'

The man on the floor was coming round and began to groan, Grigory gave him a hefty kick between the shoulder blades. 'Get your ass up, shithead.'

Jack bent down and retrieved the second man's gun. He turned to the man holding his bloodied nose. 'You've still got her keys?'

As the blood ran down his face he said something inaudible and nodded.

'Hand 'em over,' said Jack. 'Nice and easy, now.'

The lift door opened and Tom Hillman stepped out. 'Oh, no. You've started without me.'

Not wanting to be involved with any protracted police enquiry, and knowing there was a leak in the FBI, Lisa had called her controller and briefly outlined the morning's events. Her controller was already at the Capitol Building, so he'd dispatched a senior agent, along with half a dozen men, to take the suspects back to Fort Meade for interrogation. It was almost eleven o'clock when the NSA agents left Lisa's apartment with the two bloodied and decidedly unhappy assailants. As they were leaving the flat, Jack took hold of the first gunman's arm. He leaned close to the man's ear and said quietly, 'If it were up to me, I'd put a bullet in both of your heads right here.'

Chapter Forty One
'Blair House'

The President's Guest House, commonly known as Blair House, is a complex of four formerly separate buildings located at 1651 Pennsylvania Avenue. The property is owned by the United States Government for use by the President and has been called 'the world's most exclusive hotel' because it is primarily used to host visiting dignitaries, Heads of State and VIP guests. It is larger than the White House and closed to the public. Historically and traditionally, Blair House is where the President Elect spends the night before the Inauguration Ceremony.

President Elect Alex Mason and his wife Elizabeth had arrived the previous evening from his estate. For the last few days Mason had been feeling decidedly unwell. Initially believing he was suffering from a cold, he'd taken several doses of over-the-counter remedies none of which had helped. On the insistence of Elizabeth, his physician had been called to give her husband a full check-up. The doctor had prescribed painkillers for the headache and a short course of antibiotics to counter any infection. Mason had also been given a series of B12 vitamin injections.

The night however had not passed well, with a severe bout of vomiting waking him in the early hours. The doctor had been called again and a further examination found Mason to have increased blood pressure and a high temperature. After recommending three days of bed-rest, the doctor had been kicked out of the building, Mason's curses ringing in his ear.

Alex Mason was usually up by six o'clock. Rain or shine, he would run for three miles and always eat a hearty breakfast. Today he did not rise until after nine. He did not take advantage of the top of the range running machines in the gym and his appetite was zero. Although feeling poorly, he took a long shower, had a massage and drank several cups of black coffee, followed by his antibiotics and a B12 injection. He rested until ten thirty, when he got changed from his T shirt and sweat-pants into a dark blue Italian two piece suit, white linen shirt and blue silk tie. At eleven o'clock precisely a small convoy of limousines and Secret Service 4x4's pulled up to the front of Blair House.

Chapter Forty Two
'The Inauguration'

The first Presidential Inauguration was in 1789 when George Washington was sworn-in. Since the original ceremony, very little has changed, with the exception of where the actual swearing-in happens. The first twelve presidents took the oath at several different government locations but in 1837, President Martin Van Buren wanted as many Americans as possible to see the ceremony. To facilitate this, he insisted the inauguration take place on the east portico of the Capitol Building. From that day forward all inaugurations have been staged there.

The inaugural platform itself accommodates around 1600 VIP guests, including, Senators, members of Congress, Governors, members of the Diplomatic Corp, Ex-Presidents and close friends and family of the President and Vice President to be. The seating behind the main platform holds another 1000 or so people, including at least one band, several choirs, invited guests and representatives from each of the armed services. In the centre and to the front of this massive structure is a small raised platform on which the oaths are taken.

It was fifteen minutes to twelve when Vice President Elect Arthur Spencer Morgan and his wife walked down the blue carpeted steps to the front of the enormous platform. Cheers from the massed crowds and applause from the 2600 people on the platform greeted them. For a few seconds Morgan waved to the gathered masses in front of the Capitol Building and then turned as the Chief Justice of the Supreme Court joined him on the central podium. His wife Caroline stepped forward, in her hand, an original copy of the New Testament. Arthur Morgan placed his hand on the book and repeated the oath.

Sworn-in, the new Vice President waved to the people on the stands behind him, pointing to individuals and shaking hands with those around him. He turned to face the seething masses to the front and the cheering continued.

At five minutes to twelve, Vice President Morgan moved from centre stage. Behind him at the top of the blue carpeted staircase, President Elect Alex Mason and his wife Elizabeth Rhodes-Mason appeared. The crowds screamed and shouted, whistles and claxons were sounded and the massed bands played The Stars and Stripes Forever. Mason, his wife's hand in his, walked slowly down the steps, relishing and basking in the wave of adoration, the huge smile on his tanned face not giving way to the feelings of sickness he felt.

At the bottom of the steps Mason kissed his wife's cheek as she moved to the side. Her husband took up his position on the centre podium and raised his arms. The crowds went wild. Smiling and waving, he did nothing to stop the thunderous applause, until, at twelve noon precisely,the Chief Justice stepped forward once more.

Mason lowered his arms and turned to face the man next to him. Elizabeth Rhodes-Mason joined the two men; in her hands a large leather-bound copy of the St James Bible. Alex Mason smiled at his wife as he placed his left hand on the ancient tome. He raised his right hand and the crowds went silent.

In the apartment on Connecticut Avenue the four friends watched the TV in silence.

The Presidential oath took less than two minutes to be administered and affirmed. President Alex Mason continued with what seemed to be a short but rousing address and then, to the uplifting music of Hail to the Chief, the presidential party moved slowly back into the Capitol Building.

As the President re-entered the building, a smart young naval officer stepped forward, saluted and said, 'Mr President, if you would come this way for a moment, please, sir.'

The officer stood aside and indicated an open door to a small anteroom. Inside the room stood two more naval officers, resplendent in their best dress uniform. The President nodded as the first officer said, 'Please have a seat, Mr President. My name is Captain Mark Romberg, this is Lieutenant Myers and Lieutenant Grey and we are your 'football' team, sir. From this moment on and for the next four years, one of us will be within thirty seconds of you at all times.'

Open, on the table, was a compact nondescript canvas bag containing what appeared to be a small laptop type device. 'Please put your right hand on the screen, sir,' said Romberg.

One of the other officers pressed a couple of buttons on the machine and said, 'Thank you, Mr President, that's fine, sir.'

Mason removed his hand, stood up and smiled. 'Thank you, lieutenant.'

Captain Romberg handed a small leather wallet to Mason. 'These are your nuclear codes, Mr President. Please keep them on your person at all times.'

For a couple of seconds Mason looked at the object in his hand, then slipped it into his inside Jacket pocket. 'Thank you, Captain.'

'Thank you, sir.' The three officers stood to attention and simultaneously saluted. Mason raised his hand and with a serious look on his face returned the salute, then left the room.

The President and The First Lady, escorted by a large contingent of Secret Service agents left the Capitol Building via the underground parking area. A nine vehicle convoy waited to transfer them the short distance to The White House. In the sumptuous armoured limousine Elizabeth Rhodes-Mason tuned to her husband and said, 'How are you feeling, Alex?'

Mason said nothing for several seconds, as the motorised cavalcade exited the bowels of the Capitol Building and out into the bright sunshine. He patted his wife's hand and gave a weak smile. 'I'm not too bad, my dear. Just need to shake off this virus and I'll be fine.'

In Lisa's apartment Jack watched the TV coverage as the convoy travelled through the crowded streets of cheering, flag-waving Americans. 'Well, he's now the most powerful man in the world. Will he ever get what's coming to him?'

Chapter Forty Three
'Versace'

It was now almost seven in the evening. Grigory and Tom had left Lisa's place three hours earlier, their job still to provide back-up and stay undercover. Earlier in the day the NSA agent-in-charge had expressed his misgivings with regards to Lisa's two foreign friends loose in the city with weapons. Lisa however had already convinced her boss of the necessity for the covert support and, for the moment, the infraction was overlooked.

Jack had made the usual call to Nicole to assure her all was well. He had, of course omitted to report on the events in the barn and the subsequent encounter with the two would be assassins earlier in the day. His call to his brother Mathew did however include details of the attempted interrogation and intended disappearance of himself and Lisa. Mathew was intrigued how they had managed to escape their captivity, but Jack had not elaborated and certainly did not mention any support from Grigory and Tom.

Lisa was already waiting for him in the sitting room. 'My, my, Mr Castle. Don't you scrub up well?'

He grinned as he straitened the bow tie. 'Why thank you, ma'am. And may I say how wonderfully elegant you are looking in your Versace.'

Lisa smiled, not surprised he recognised the designer gown. 'How's the suit fit?'

Jack looked down and fastened the single button on the Jacket. He adjusted the sliver of white handkerchief in the breast pocket and said, 'Fits fine. It's a great evening suit, considering it's hired.'

'Okay then, hun. Shall we go to the ball?'

He offered his arm and she hooked her hand under his elbow. 'Yes, ma'am.'

Chapter Forty Four
'Mr Vice President'

In 1974 the United States Government permanently assigned a house on the southeast corner of 34th Street and Massachusetts Avenue. The three storey, Victorian style building sits within the grounds of the United States Naval Observatory, and, while in office, is the residence of the American Vice President.

Arthur Spencer Morgan smiled at his reflection in the full length mirror and said, 'Mr Vice President,' he said it again, this time with his shoulders back and head turned slightly to the left. 'Mr Vice President.' He laughed at himself as he continued to get dressed, the cufflinks that once belonged to his grandfather, as always, causing him a problem as he tried to insert them into the stiff cuffs of his new evening shirt. Frustrated, and not wanting to get annoyed with himself, he left his dressing room and walked next door to his wife's room. 'Caroline, I'm sorry, my dear, these cufflinks again.' He held out his hands like a small child waiting to be helped by his mother.

The elegant woman stood up from the dressing table, smiled lovingly at her husband and said, 'Come here.'

As she deftly inserted the troublesome pieces of silver, he said, 'You look lovely, my darling.'

She straightened the cuffs then stepped back to look at her husband. She reached up and adjusted his bowtie, then gently touched his cheek. 'Mr Vice President. I love you.'

He leaned down and kissed her forehead, then said, 'What's this?' as he picked up a small black flash-stick from the table.

Caroline said, 'Oh, that. Emily Harding-West introduced me to an old friend of hers at the *Daughters* lunch the other day. We chatted for a few minutes and she gave me that. She said I should pass it on to you as it contained something extremely important.'

'But you didn't?'

'My dear, you have so much to do that is important. I was going to give it to you later.'

He smiled and kissed her again on the forehead. 'Are you nearly ready?'

'Yes, I'll be down in a few minutes. Shall we be naughty and have a cocktail before we go?'

He grinned, 'Why not? I am the Vice President.'

As he walked down the sweeping staircase he looked at the flash-stick. At the bottom of the stairs he crossed the hallway and went into the study. The laptop was open on the desk and he quickly inserted the device. He watched for several minutes until his wife entered the room. 'Arthur, what are you doing? I thought we were having cocktails?'

The Vice President looked up, his face ashen. 'You need to see this.'

Chapter Forty Five
'Mr President'

After arriving at The White House, President Alex Mason had gone directly to the Oval Office, where several of his top advisors were already waiting to greet him. Although he had not yet confirmed his inner cabinet, many of his intended inner circle already knew who would be in the administration.

His very first task was to formally sign and send a presidential signal to each of America's nuclear ballistic missile submarines. These signals were confirmation to the sub commanders that Alexander Stonewall Mason was now their Commander-in-Chief. Several other similar signals were sent to various high-ranking members of the military, confirming the appointment. This formality over, he thanked the gathered officials and diplomats, left the Oval Office and made his way to his residence in the central part of the building.

There were over a dozen people moving the last of the Mason's personal furniture and effects into the lounge when the President arrived. His wife quickly thanked and dismissed the staff and once all had departed said, 'How are you feeling, Alex?'

Mason loosened his tie and slumped down on the big couch. 'Could you get me a brandy please, my dear.'

'I don't think you should take alcohol with the medication.'

'Just a small one. Please?'

She went to the cabinet and found the cognac, poured a miniscule amount into a brandy balloon and handed it to her husband. 'That's all you're having.'

Mason smiled weakly and then swallowed the drink in one. He coughed several times as the strong alcohol caught his throat. Elizabeth took the empty glass. 'I know you won't rest properly today but after this evening is over, I really do want you to have a few days to get rid of this virus.'

'I will, my dear, I will. I'll take another B12 shot and then go and have a nap for a couple of hours. I'll be fine for tonight. You finish doing whatever it is you're doing in here. Just don't let me sleep too long, please.'

She reached up, touched his check and kissed him. 'Whatever you say, Mr President.'

Chapter Forty Six
'The Inaugural Ball'

In the foyer of the Potomac Hilton, Jack and Lisa joined the considerable queue for the security screening. Several conveyor scanners had been temporarily installed and polite but efficient security personnel directed the guests as they arrived. Handbags, wallets, phones, keys were placed onto small trays and passed through the x-ray machines as each guest walked through a detector, the odd beep and flashing light causing the queue to come to a halt, as someone failed to remove an item.

Once through security, the guests were directed to a large anteroom in order to have their ID's confirmed. Two dozen tables were staffed by attractive young aides, each checking identities and collating names with the computerised guest list. After showing their invitations and photographic ID, a bar-coded band was placed on their wrist and as they left the anteroom the wrist-bands were scanned, by yet another security officer. Jack waited for Lisa to come out then said quietly, 'Just like getting into Glastonbury.'

She shook her head slightly and linked her arm with his. 'Yes, but the mud around here is not underfoot, honey.'

On entering the main ballroom they checked the huge seating plan and identified their table. The elegant room was filling up quickly, wine was already flowing, and on each table guests chatted excitedly, their voices mixed with the sound of jazz tunes coming from the fabulous orchestra.

'Here we are,' she said as they approached a large circular table with a dozen seats around it. Three couples were already seated but the men stood up as Lisa and Jack introduced themselves. Lisa was impressed by the table's centrepiece, an elaborate floral arrangement reputedly fashioned with flowers from Mason's own estate, above which and completely destroying the classy arrangement, floated several red, white and blue balloons. A waiter quickly appeared and poured Lisa a glass of Champagne, Jack's hand over his champagne flute stopped the waiter serving him the same. 'Just sparkling water, please.'

Jack looked around the huge ballroom. He'd been to many society events with Nicole but this place was definitely in a class of its own. Washington's glitterati were certainly out in force tonight. The most glamourous people, in their most elegant clothes, where anyone who was anyone, came together every eight years for the most prestigious event in the capitol's calendar, The Inaugural Gala.

The room was packed with the good and the great of DC's political, military and business world. The sixty-piece orchestra played while the champagne and wine flowed in unashamed celebration. The dance floor was already crowded as dozens of couples swayed to the wonderful sound of the country's top orchestra. Liveried waiting staff kept the crystal flutes topped with Moet

Chandon as quickly as they were emptied, and the party atmosphere permeated every inch of the luxurious hotel.

'What are you smiling about?' said Lisa quietly.

Jack leaned-in closer. 'I've never seen so many sycophants in one room before.'

She shook her head. 'Behave,' then took hold of his hand. 'Come on I want to dance before it all goes political.'

By the time they returned to the table, Emily Harding-West and her husband, Congressman James West had arrived.

Seeing her friend, Emily jumped up and kissed Lisa on both cheeks. 'Darling, it's wonderful you're here tonight,' then quietly into her ear continued, 'otherwise I'd be stuck with this bunch of old fuddy-duddies.'

Lisa smiled. 'Lovely to see you too, Emily. This is my friend Jack Castle. Jack, this is my very good friend, Emily Harding-West and her husband, Congressman James West.'

Jack smiled and shook hands with the Congressman then turned to Emily. 'Pleased to meet you, Emily. Lisa's told me all about you.'

The handshake lasted several seconds, then Emily said, 'Well, she certainly has not told me anything about you, Jack,' then looking at Lisa said, 'where have you been keeping him, darling?'

Lisa raised her eyebrows slightly and said, 'Let's have a seat, shall we.'

As they took their seats, Lisa squeezed Jack's arm as several Secret Service men quickly lined up in front of the stage. The dance music stopped and was replaced by cheers and clapping, as Mason's Campaign Director walked up to the podium. The cheering from the crowd continued as he shouted into the mic, 'Is everyone ready for a great night?'

He raised his arms, Moses-like, to calm the gathered throng and the noise abated.

'Senators, Congressmen, esteemed guests, ladies and gentlemen, please welcome . . . The President of the United States of America, Alexander Stonewall Mason.'

The crowd screamed and applauded as the orchestra struck up 'Hail to the Chief' and then went wild, as Alex Mason swaggered onto the stage.

At the podium, Mason stood and looked out at the adoring crowd before him, a huge smile across his tanned face. He waited for almost two minutes as his frenzied supporters screamed, cheered and applauded, then raised a hand and stepped towards the microphone. 'Friends, Americans, Countrymen.' again the crowd went wild as he paraphrased Mark Anthony.

Jack put his mouth close to Lisa's ear. 'What a fucking arsehole.'

Turning, she smiled. 'Shush,' then looked back to the man on stage.

Mason waved his hand and the audience calmed. 'My friends, tonight we celebrate. Tomorrow we renew our country.'

More cheering and clapping and again the hand was raised. 'Thank you . . . Thank you all. And now let me introduce the man who will work at my side. My friend and your Vice President, Arthur Spencer Morgan.'

The Vice President walked slowly onto the stage, the standing crowds cheered and clapped wildly. Jack watched as the man halted and raised his arm, something in his hand glinted in the bright spotlights.

Mason, surprised, looked at his running mate and then, realising what was about to happen, raised his hand as if to shield himself. The gunshot was not that loud in the huge crowd-filled auditorium. Morgan's first bullet took the third and fourth fingers from Mason's raised hand, the second round entered the muscle high on the shoulder, knocking the startled President to the floor.

Screams and more gunshots but this time from the Secret Service as they rushed the platform. Their deadly volley thumping into Morgan's chest, knocking him backwards onto the white carpeted stage.

Pandemonium from the crowd, as half a dozen agents now covered the cowering figure of Alex Mason. Then, as one, like a Roman shield wall, they used their bodies to protect and rush him off the stage and out of harm's way.

The second group of agents were now up on the stage, arms outstretched, weapons pointed. They circled the dying body of the Vice President. One agent kicked the small chrome plated revolver away from Morgan's hand and then knelt down next to him, feeling for a pulse. Blood oozed from the chest wounds turning the new evening shirt deep scarlet. He coughed weakly and his mouth filled with blood, spilling out it ran down both sides of his face and onto the white carpet. A crimson halo formed around Morgan's head as he said a single, almost inaudible word, 'Justice.'

Chapter Forty Seven
'Full and Complete Recovery'

The following morning the internet, news agencies, TV and newspapers all over the world, ran nothing other than the assassination attempt on the American President. Speculation as to why the Vice President had committed such an appalling act was rife.

The shocking news however was counterbalanced by positive reports on Alex Mason's condition. The President had sustained an injury to his hand which had resulted in the loss of two fingers. The wound to his upper arm would not however leave any long term damage. He was in a stable condition, although there were concerns he may have succumbed to an infection that was slowing his recovery.

The Surgeon General had been in attendance at all times and had issued a statement saying he expected the President to make a full and complete recovery. A senior presidential aide had also made an upbeat statement on TV, announcing the President himself had confirmed he intends to be in the White House by the end of the week. For the moment The Speaker of the House was currently standing in until President Mason returned.

All the information being fed to the media was accurate, with one exception. The doctors were not happy with the virus the President had succumbed to. His wife had told them her husband had been suffering from a strong cold or virus for several days prior to the inauguration and if anything it seemed to be getting worse, not better.

Chapter Forty Eight
'Dasvidanya'

Dulles International is one of three major airports serving the Baltimore-Washington area and with over twenty-one million passengers a year, handles more international travellers than any other airport on the east coast, with the exception of New York.

It had been over thirty-six hours since President Mason had been shot by Arthur Spencer Morgan. At the airport the newspapers, televisions, passengers and staff spoke about nothing else. Speculation still ran riot as to why the shooting happened and how the Vice President managed to actually do the deed. The reports coming from Walter Reed Medical Hospital were not encouraging either, and it appeared the doctors were fighting to control the President's septicaemia.

The morning was a little overcast as Lisa drove Jack out to Dulles. By the time they'd parked up, passed the outer security and into the main Departures Concourse, it was almost seven o'clock. Jack's plane was not until midday but Tom was booked on the 09:30 Emirates flight to Dubai. The huge hall was packed but as they'd agreed to meet at O'Leary's Irish Bar, it was a simple matter of pushing through the crowds to the popular traveller's watering hole.

Tom and Grigory were seated in the far corner of the busy pub. Grigory stood and waved when he saw Lisa and Jack enter. The four friends all hugged and Lisa planted kisses on the cheeks of Tom and Grigory.

'You want some drink?' asked the big Russian.

'I'd love a coffee, hun.'

Jack shook his head as Grigory pushed his way to the bar.

'Do we know what the latest is with Mason?' said Tom.

Jack shrugged his shoulders. 'They're saying he has a problem with septicaemia but to me that sounds like it's come on pretty quick.'

'They must have done blood tests to confirm his condition though?' said Lisa.

'Who knows?' said Jack. 'The man's sick but is probably gonna recover. And all he'll have lost is a couple of fingers. His approval rating will probably increase after being shot.'

'Coffee,' said Grigory, passing the mug to Lisa. 'Cream no sugar. Right?'

'Thanks, honey.'

'Okay, guys. I'd better make a move.' said Tom, as he picked up his holdall.

Lisa put her drink down, hugged Tom and said, 'Thank you for all you did. I still wish I'd known you were here from the start but that's his fault.' She cocked her thumb at Jack.

'Was great to see you again, Lisa. Get yourself over to Dubai, spend some time on the yacht.'

'I will. I promise, Tom.'

Tom turned to the Russian. 'Grigory, my friend. It's been fun. Give my regards to your brother Bogdan when he gets out. You both need to come down to the Gulf as well, eh?'

The big man hugged Tom. 'Da, da, was fun. Sure, I see you in Gulf sometime. If not, you come to Moscow. Dasvidanya, Tominski.'

Jack and Tom walked to the exit of the bar. 'Cheers, buddy. Saved my arse again.'

Tom grinned. 'We're a team. We look after each other. But next time I save your arse can you have some bloody clothes on, please?'

They both laughed.

An hour later Lisa and Jack walked Grigory to the Departures Security. The same goodbyes were enacted when the big Russian left to catch the Aeroflot flight to Moscow. As he disappeared through the scanner area Jack said, 'You want a bit of breakfast before I shove off, babe?'

She linked her arm with his and said, 'Sure.'

On the mezzanine level they found a more up-market and decidedly quieter venue than the Irish bar. Once seated in the pleasant dining room they ordered breakfast.

'Have you called Nicole yet?' said Lisa.

'I'll ring her once I get on board.'

As the waitress brought their hot drinks, a murmur rippled around the restaurant. People were looking at their smartphones and a woman at the next table said out loud, 'Oh. no!'

Lisa took out her phone and swiped the screen. 'Oh, my God. He's dead, Jack. The President is dead.'

Chapter Forty Nine
'First Class Lounge'

It was a few minutes before ten when they arrived at the entrance to Departures Security.

'Thanks, Lisa, you're a star,' said Jack.

She kissed his cheek and hugged him. 'One of these days we'll all get together for some real fun.'

He frowned. 'Don't we have fun now?'

She slapped his arm lightly. 'You know what I mean.'

'Sure. Come over to London soon, eh? Nicole is dying to see you. And I am always happy to see you, babe.'

She reached up and kissed his cheek again. 'I will. I promise. Now get outta here, handsome.'

Jack winked. 'See you soon, gorgeous.'

She watched as he entered the scanner. As he came out the other side he turned and waved. She blew a kiss, then put her hand over her heart.

The arduous and rigorous security checks over, Jack found himself in the First Class lounge with an hour to spare before his flight. He took out his smartphone and checked emails and messages, several of which were from his brother Mathew. He swiped the screen and listened for the connection to be made.

'Jack, hi. Haven't heard from you for a couple of days. Everything okay?'

'Yeah, I'm fine, Matt. Leaving soon, back this evening.'

'We're just watching the news. So, Mason has died?'

'Yeah. They say it was sepsis. But who knows? I'll come in tomorrow and we can catch up, if that's okay, bro.'

'Sure, Jack. You have a good flight. See you soon.'

Jack stared at the blank screen for several seconds, until a voice made him look up.

'Jack Castle. Good to see you again,' said Vanya Kuragin. 'Okay if I join you?'

Jack looked at the immaculately dressed mafia boss. 'Sure, why not? Where you headed, Vanya?'

The Russian winked salaciously. 'I have a little business in London.'

'So you're on the BA flight?'

'Da, we are travelling companions. Yes?'

Jack raised an eyebrow. 'I guess so. Where are your minders, Vanya?'

The young man grinned. 'Where you think? They travel Business not First.'

Jack laughed a little and said, 'And how is Uncle Sasha?'

'He's very well and very happy with today's news.'

Under his breath Jack said, 'Aren't we all?'

Vanya leaned forward across the low table and said quietly, 'So how you manage to get the Vice President to shoot Mason, Jack?'

Jack looked the man straight in the eyes. 'What makes you think I had anything to do with that?'

The Russian sat back and grinned. 'Because you believe in justice, my friend.'

'Yeah, maybe.'

Vanya leaned back over the table his voice low again. 'We also believe in justice but most of all we believe in revenge.'

'Whatever you say, Vanya.'

A waitress appeared and asked if they needed anything.

'I'll have glass of Champagne,' said the Russian.

Jack raised his hand and smiled. 'Nothing thank you, sweetie.'

The girl left and Vanya again lowered his voice. 'But your efforts did not succeed, eh, Jack?'

Jack leaned forward this time. 'You're right he didn't die from his wounds but the infection did the job in the end.'

The waitress arrived with Vanya's Champagne. 'Anything else, gentlemen?'

As she walked away the Russian picked up the crystal flute, drank half its contents and said, 'I love Champagne.'

Jack grinned. 'Of course you do. I can tell you're a connoisseur.'

Vanya placed the glass on the table, then leaned in again. 'But it was not your virus that killed him, Jack.'

Jack frowned and said quietly. 'What the fuck you on about, Vanya?'

The young mafia boss smiled. 'Have you ever heard of the *Baby's Egg*? The one Faberge made?'

Chapter Fifty
'Goodbye, Vanya'

Thankfully Vanya Kuragin was at the opposite end of the First Class Cabin, so Jack did not have to engage too much with the young Russian and the eight hour flight passed reasonably well, with Jack managing to get a few hours of sleep.

At Heathrow's First Class arrival's Jack was treated to more of the Russian's inane jokes, but once through Immigration and Customs, their ways parted and Jack hurriedly made his way to the Arrivals Hall and a waiting Nicole.

He could see her waving from the exit door and Jack pushed his way through the waiting crowd to his beautiful wife.

'Zaikin,' she said, as she threw her arms around his neck.

His words were cut off as her lips crushed into his.

'Did you miss me?' said Jack when they eventually came up for air.

'All the time, Jack. All the time.'

He kissed her again, then said, 'Okay, let's get home.'

As they left the terminal building a long black limousine pulled up at the kerb. 'This isn't for us? Is it?' said Jack.

Before he could answer a burly gentleman pushed past and opened the rear door.

'Niet, Jack. This is mine,' said Kuragin, as he looked Nicole up and down.

Jack grinned. 'Goodbye, Vanya. Look after yourself.'

'You not gonna introduce us, Jack?'

As they walked away Jack said again, 'Goodbye, Vanya. Take care.'

The Russian laughed. 'You too my friend. Dasvidanya.'

It was almost ten o'clock in the evening when they arrived home to East Monkton. The twins had been put to bed several hours earlier but Svetlana had waited up until she knew Jack and Nicole had returned. After the nanny had gone, Nicole said, 'Do you want anything, Zaikin? Some tea?'

Jack shook his head. 'Just a shower and then bed, darling.'

She kissed him and linked her arm under his. 'Sounds perfect.'

Chapter Fifty One
'Endings

Jack arrived at Vauxhall House a little before noon. His brother Mathew was in a meeting when Jack entered the outer office.

'Good morning, Mr Castle. Nice to see you again, sir,' said Mathew's secretary.

'Hello, Victoria. You okay?'

'Fine, sir. Bit of a flap on this morning but he shouldn't be too long. He's expecting you.   Can I get you anything to drink, sir?'

'No thank you, sweetie.'

Jack had been waiting for almost thirty-five minutes when several people left Mathew's office. Mathew came to the door and said, 'Sorry Jack. Come in, please. Hold my calls, please, Victoria.'

'Yes, sir.'

'How was your flight, Jack?'

'Was ok, bro. You seem to have a bit of a problem today?'

Mathew sat down behind his desk. 'Have a seat. Yeah. We've had some reports from our cousins across the pond. Got a few of our people on the tops floors knicker's in a twist.'

'Oh, yeah. About what?'

'They did an immediate post-mortem on Mason yesterday. We've been made privy to the results by our friends in the CIA.'

Jack sat forward in his seat. 'So I'm guessing he didn't die from sepsis?'

Mathew shook his head slightly, stood up and went to the window. 'What do you know about Polonium-210, Jack?'

Jack looked at his brother. 'It's pretty dangerous stuff. Highly radioactive and allegedly the most toxic substance known to man. Apparently there's no cure if you're exposed to it.'

Mathew turned back from the window. 'That's right, Jack.'

* * *

It was still early morning on The Magnolia Estate and the Government HAZMAT teams had been searching the house for over an hour and a half. In the library, two specialists, dressed from head to toe in protective suits, were methodically scanning every inch of the elegant room. As one of the team approached the huge fireplace his Geiger-counter immediately responded, the ticking becoming faster and louder the nearer he came.

'Here we go,' he shouted to his companion.

They both moved in on the source of the signal and then, as the first specialist raised his scanner to the centre of the mantle, the noise from the machine became high pitched and constant. The specialist looked at the small display. 'Jesus, look at this! It's off the charts.'

They switched off their equipment and stood back, looking at a beautiful Fabergé egg.

Within the hour the FBI had broken down the front door of Senator David Ashton's river-side home in Georgetown. The twelve man SWAT team however were not required, as they found the Senator already dead, due to what appeared to be a cocaine overdose.

* * *

On the sixth floor of The Washington Post building, the meeting was definitely heating up. Gerry Conway, the paper's senior editor, stood and looked through the window to the busy street below. 'This is gonna be the biggest story since the Kennedy assassination.'

'Bigger,' said Lisa.

'I need to take this to the board.'

Lisa stood and joined her boss at the window. 'Gerry, are you the editor or not?'

'Alexander Mason was a respected general and war hero. He'd just been elected to the presidency for God sake.'

'He was also a conspirator, a thief and a murderer,' said Lisa, 'and has just been assassinated by what appears to be Polonium poisoning. Does this story need to get any bigger before you run it, Gerry? Jesus, man, have some balls. You're gonna have the biggest story in the world, before any other news-source.'

Conway turned back to the window and for several seconds watched the people on the crowded street below. 'You're right. The people need to know the truth. Write the story, Lisa, we'll both get a Pulitzer.'

The End

Epilogue

Jack's young entrepreneur friend sold his application to Google for $7.2 million. When they offered him a position with their design team, he politely refused and said he was working on a new application that would enable people to make payments with their smartphone.

When Grigory returned to Moscow, he was happy to find his brother Bogdan was recovering from the Lubyanka beating. He was still in a secure hospital ward but thanks to a phone call from Dimitri Orlov, Grigory was allowed to visit. Two hours were spent as Grigory went through the events in America and, leaving nothing out, was not surprised when Bogdan said, 'Tell me again how you rescued a naked Lisa from the barn.'

Tom travelled back to the Emirates and was met at the airport by his wife Helen. She was delighted and amazed to find, after another mission with Jack Castle, her husband had managed to return home without any injuries or scars.

In the apartment overlooking Central Park, Sasha Ivanovich Kuragin read the newspaper report on the tragic death of President Alex Mason. The paper went into detail on how the doctors had fought to save him from the severe case of septicaemia, which had regrettably developed from wounds he'd sustained at the Inaugural Gala. Kuragin smiled, put the paper down and went out onto the balcony. As he looked out over the lush green park, he said quietly, 'Alexei my brother, you have now been avenged.'

Vice President Morgan's wife Caroline was arrested on charges of conspiracy to murder the President. Thankfully, as there was no proof she colluded with her dead husband and with considerable pressure from her socially elite friends, the charges were swiftly dropped. But not before she was forced to offer a reason as to why her husband might want to murder the President. In the interview the senior FBI agent asked her to explain.

'In 2005 our child was killed in Afghanistan. Flight Lieutenant Sam Morgan's plane was shot down as it took off from Kabul.'

'So your husband believed President Mason, General Mason at that time, had something to do with the death of your son?'

With tears in her eyes she looked at the man across from her. 'Not my son. My daughter. Her name was Samantha, but she always used Sam.'

A special delivery arrived at Lisa's apartment, the postmark, Bresica, Italy. On opening the package she found an elegantly produced brochure showing the specification of the Beretta DT11 Shotgun. Also in the package was an open First Class air ticket to Italy and

217

information about accommodation on the banks of Lake Garda, a few kilometres away from Bresica. An envelope with the Beretta Company logo was address to Miss Lisa Reynard and inside a hand-written note, which said:

Dear Miss Reynard.

One of our finest guns has been purchased for you and at your convenience is awaiting your arrival, at which time we will be delighted to fit the gun to your personal specification.

Mr Castle wishes to be advised when you intend to travel, as he and his lady wife would be delighted to join you in Italy.

We look forward to seeing you in the not too distant future.

Yours Sincerely,

Giovani Marcello Fabrizi.

Director, The Beretta Armaments Company, Bresica.

Jack Castle will be back . . .